Our Time on the River

Our Time on the River

DON BROWN

HOUGHTON
MIFFLIN
COMPANY
BOSTON 2003

Library of Congress Cataloging-in-Publication Data
Brown, Don.
Our time on the river / by Don Brown.
p. cm.
Summary: Two brothers take a river trip by canoe in advance
of the elder brother being shipped out to Vietnam.
ISBN 0-618-31116-5
[1. Brothers—Fiction. 2. Canoes and canoeing—Fiction.
3. Rivers—Fiction.] I. Title.
PZ7.B81295 Ou 2003   [Fic]—dc21   2002015325

Manufactured in the United States of America
QUM 10 9 8 7 6 5 4 3 2 1

For Evan

1

The December night brought more than snow.

A thumping at the kitchen door drew Dad, Mom, and me from different rooms in our house, and we met at its threshold. There stood David, stamping clusters of wet snow from his boots.

"Sweetheart!" Mom exclaimed. "Quick, get out of the cold."

My brother's arrival on that snowy evening wasn't a surprise. Although he was enrolled at a state college near Syracuse, many weekends found him at home, spending much of his time with Dad. My parents said he was suffering from homesickness.

"Gotta get my stuff," David said with a smile.

He dragged in two suitcases, an ancient steamer trunk, several cardboard boxes sealed with masking tape, and a plastic garbage bag that spilled clothes when David dropped it to the floor. Mom and Dad just stared at it all.

"How come you brought all your stuff home?" I finally asked.

"Is something wrong? Did something happen at college..." Dad stammered.

"I enlisted," he said.

"You..." Dad replied.

"What do you mean, you 'enlisted'?" Mom asked, her voice hard and sharp.

"I wasn't getting anything out of college. Joined the army. Enlisted. I thought—"

"The army! There is a war on. A war!" Mom shouted. "Tell them you've made a mistake. Tell them you're not enlisting! You're not going to Vietnam!"

Mom turned to Dad and said, "Go with him. Explain it was a mistake. Tell them he is not enlisting!"

"Calm down! Wait a second! Let me...you..." Dad stuttered, then took a deep breath. "Tell me what you did. Exactly. You enlisted? In the regular army, not ROTC. The regular army?"

David threw up his hands and shouted, "Yes! The regular army! Geez, I thought *you'd* understand. You said you're proud of the guys in Nam."

"You discussed this?" Mom cried, and she stepped in front of Dad. "And you didn't tell me! You approved."

"I didn't approve. We talked...I thought..." Dad said.

"You let him enlist? During a war?" Mom yelled.

"I told him to finish school!" Dad said. He turned his attention to David. "What will you learn in the army? To sleep in a hole, a ditch? To—"

2

"I never would have given my permission!" Mom interrupted.

"I didn't..." Dad said.

"I didn't get Dad's permission. I didn't get anybody's permission. I did it on my own. It was my decision!" David barked.

"You don't know!" Mom cried.

"It'll be OK," Dad said, speaking more to himself than us. "He's a smart kid. They'll probably give him some kind of technical job, or an office job. A no-fighting job. A noncombatant. It'll be OK. Maybe it'll be good for him. Help him mature. Let's try to make the best—"

"Good for him?" Mom exclaimed. "Oh, God! Like it was good for Dee?"

Dee was Mom's brother, who had died in World War II. Mom had spoken of him many times. Dad dropped his hands, and his shoulders slumped. Mom crossed her arms and glared at him.

"Gee, thanks for killing me off, Mom!" David shouted. He grabbed the steamer trunk and stomped out of the kitchen and up to his room.

"David!" Mom called.

I picked up a suitcase and followed him upstairs. I could hear Mom and Dad arguing in the kitchen. David was sitting on his bed when I got there. His face was red with anger.

"Dad wasn't much older than me when he was in the army!" David yelled, startling me. "It's OK for him, but not me?"

I didn't know what to say.

3

"I can go to college anytime. When I'm a middle-aged guy, I don't want to look back and kick myself in the ass for missing a war," he said.

"It looks scary," I offered. "On TV."

"Nobody's asking you to join," he snapped.

"I just—"

"What do *you* know? Why don't you go downstairs with them."

"I—"

"Get out of my room!"

"Wh—"

"GET OUT OF MY ROOM! Freaking twerp!"

"Screw you!" I screamed.

Dad marched in, grabbed me by the back of the neck, and steered me into the hall.

"Get to your room, Steven!" he said, and he closed David's door behind him. Mom stood at the foot of the stairs, her eyes fastened on the shut door. Dad argued with David for the next half hour.

Two weeks later, David departed for army basic training.

2

The light from a bright spring day flooded the kitchen. I ate breakfast at the counter and watched Saturday morning cartoons on a tiny portable TV. Mom loaded the washing machine, ignoring the banging of the dryer as it spinned an unbalanced load. We didn't hear David's arrival, and Mom and I jumped when he shouted, "Hey, I'm home."

He stood in the dining room, which adjoined the kitchen. A madras shirt draped his muscular, barrel-chested frame. His hair was cut very short, contrary to the popular style.

Mom raced over and hugged him. He looked over her shoulder at me and said, "Hey, loser, what's going on?"

I winced and didn't say anything.

Mom let go of David slowly. She bombarded him with questions: was he eating, did he need his clothes laundered, was everything OK at Fort Belvoir? David edged me away from the counter and took my seat. Mom whisked away my unfinished breakfast and dropped the leftovers into the trash. David settled in and answered Mom's barrage of questions.

The front door opened and Dad arrived. He had been fishing and was carrying a huge bluefish.

"David!" he roared when he saw his oldest son. "Great fishing today! One guy got five big ones! I got this monster," he said, and he dropped the fish in the sink. "Did you just get home?" He clasped David's shoulders, examined him from head to toe, and smiled. Then he hooked my neck into his elbow and pulled me close to the two of them.

Mom moved to the sink, brushing against us as she passed. She gingerly used two fingers to lift the fish by its tail and lay it down on a newspaper she had spread on the counter.

Dad merrily began to entertain us with the tale of the huge bluefish and its capture. David and I laughed; I barely noticed the drone of the TV, the thump of the clothes in the dryer, or the soft metallic chatter of a knife scraping fish scales.

At the end of his story, Dad clapped his hands and asked, "How are you?"

Before David could answer, the telephone rang.

"That must be Ken. I told him I was coming home and to phone now," David explained. He rushed to his bedroom and took the call from his best high school friend.

"I guess that's all we're gonna see of that kid!" Dad said in mock exasperation.

Mom smiled.

Dad said, "Let's have ice cream for dessert tonight. Come on, Steve. Take a ride with me."

We headed to the store in our big Ford Country Squire station wagon. I jabbered about fishing, friends, and how scared I was of starting high school in the fall. Although my father had been in a brighter mood just moments earlier, he was now silent and expressionless. Without warning, he steered the car into the parking lot of a drugstore and shut off the engine.

"David is destined to go to Vietnam," he said evenly. "He told me a couple of weeks ago. His orders have him leaving in the middle of September out of McGuire Air Force Base. He thinks he can angle a long leave before going, so he should be around for the month of August. He came home today to break the news to your mother. He plans to tell her at dinner."

Dad measured my response for a moment. Then, without further comment, he started the car and drove off.

I sat mute. My mind went to the *Life* magazine that was stuffed in a rack in our den. In it were the photos of every American killed in Vietnam the previous week—287.

"Destined" rang in my mind.

We sat down for dinner at six o'clock. The sound of the evening news on the TV carried easily into the dining room. Dad and David were already seated at our antique oval table when I entered. Mom fussed in the kitchen.

"Did I say it was OK to wear that?" David asked, eyeing the maroon sweatshirt with a giant gray "1967" on the front. It had been awarded to him at his high school graduation the previous year. I think the thick, soft sweatshirt meant more to him than his diploma.

Before I could answer, Mom carried a platter of fish and pasta to the table. "Here we are," she chirped, placing it in front of Dad. He quickly served himself a huge portion. The platter made its way to David and then to me. Finally, Mom set a tiny portion of fish on her plate.

"The Wayne boy got into medical school. Cornell, I think," Mom said, and she began to dispense news about our neighbors: a medical-school admission for the Waynes, a pregnancy for the Lotellis, a home improvement project for the Fishers. She neglected to mention the divorce for the LaTorrances, the bypass surgery for the Bronskys, and the traffic accident for the Roths.

Halfway through Mom's news about the Spiveys' new puppy, Dad narrowed his eyes and glanced at David. David quickly swallowed the food in his mouth, pushed his fork aside, and sat up straight.

"Mom," David said gently.

She stopped talking. She smiled and her eyes danced, but only for an instant. Like an animal that can sense an impending earthquake, she seemed to feel the world shifting beneath her. Her smile melted.

"I have to go to Vietnam," he said slowly. "In September."

Mom sat up straight and momentarily strangled on a gulp of air. She quickly brought her napkin to her face to meet the tears that were already leaking from her eyes. I was frozen in my chair. Dad said nothing and did not move. David got out of his seat and went to her.

"It'll be OK, Ma. I'm gonna try to get headquarters duty,"

David said. "I'll probably spend the whole tour in Saigon, in an office, an air-conditioned office. It's gonna be OK. I promise. I promise."

Mom wrapped her arms about herself. She stared at the half-eaten fish. Her eyes were liquid and her brow was knotted. What was she thinking? That the war would ignore David's promises and his survival or death would be delivered as if by whim? Or had her mind leaped back more than twenty-five years to World War II?

David and I had heard the story often. How Dad had been sprayed by a German machine gun the morning of his first day of combat. How a slug blasted his boot and carried away his pinky toe. How more bullets hit him in the buttocks, thigh, and ankle before he hit the ground. David and I had seen the half dozen purple-pink scars and how Dad limped when he walked.

The day Mom received the War Department telegram about Dad's injuries, her younger brother Dee was struck by American bombs dropped on the wrong target. He was blown to bits and returned home in a coffin that the army made sure couldn't be opened.

Dee was his nickname. His real name was David, and he was my brother's namesake.

3

I lay sprawled on the sugar-fine Jones Beach sand and faced the ocean. My eyes drifted to the horizon. I was neatly sandwiched between night and day. To the east, the dawning sky was a brilliant cobalt-blue. To the west, the remnants of night were a sober Prussian blue. The onshore breeze carried the noise of crashing waves; it sounded like cannons.

Dad and David stood in the gentle surf. Dad whipped his long surf-casting rod forward, hurling a glittering lure into small waves that were breaking against a sandbar fifty yards offshore. He and David laughed. I couldn't hear what they were saying. Dad tilted his head toward me. David's smile vanished, and he started speaking rapidly. Dad shook his head several times. David's shoulders slumped, his arms fell to his sides, and he stared out to sea. Dad reeled in the line, shifted the rod to one hand, and firmly gripped David's shoulder with the other, directing him to shore. David fell in behind Dad and the two trudged through the water toward me.

When they reached me, Dad smiled and announced, "David's gonna take you down the Susquehanna."

The Susquehanna River. As a teenager, Dad had once canoed its length: Cooperstown, New York, to Havre de Grace, Maryland. He touted the experience as "man building." After David turned thirteen, Dad and he spent summer holidays canoeing sections of the river. They came home smelling of mildew, pine cones, and sweat.

By the time I turned thirteen, Dad had discovered surfcast fishing. We'd drive to the beach at dawn, when the sun was just a pale ocher-colored disk. I'd help carry the tackle box and fish buckets to the shore. I told Dad things I could never find the words for at home. Talking came easier for me at the beach, and Dad listened better, too. I helped land the occasional catch, but mostly I'd swim. The tossing, turning ocean frightened me at first, but in time my fear diminished. I even taught myself to bodysurf, and I became an expert at sliding down the face of a wave. Still, I never learned to canoe.

"David only has a couple of weeks to spare, so you won't have a prayer of making Havre de Grace," Dad said. "Maybe you can make it into Pennsylvania, above Wilkes-Barre. I'll explain the plan to your mother."

"This is Dad's idea," David added. I wasn't sure if he was complaining or explaining.

That evening, I lay in the dark and listened to Mom and

Dad talk in the adjoining bedroom. The wall separating us muffled their conversation, until their voices became sharper.

"David says he doesn't want to go," Mom said.

"He's doing it as a favor to me. I told him it's important for Stevie to spend time with him," Dad answered.

"Did you speak with Steve?"

I couldn't make out Dad's answer.

After a few moments, Mom asked, "Where are they going to sleep?"

"They'll camp out."

"I don't like it," she continued. "It's dangerous."

Silence.

"Well, isn't it?"

"No," Dad answered in a strong voice. "They'll be fine. David can take care of things."

More silence.

"You said he wouldn't be sent—"

"I said I *thought* he wouldn't be sent," Dad snapped. "They taught him to type. I thought he'd end up doing clerical work in the States. I thought—"

"You thought! You thought! He's going to Vietnam!" Mom cried.

A long silence.

"He's eighteen. He enlisted. We couldn't have stopped him," Dad said.

The silence returned, and I fell asleep.

4

A brisk wind blew across Otsego Lake and into my face. Small choppy waves splashed over the bow of the canoe and into my lap. Behind me, David barked instructions: "Paddle harder! Paddle on both sides! Don't shift your weight suddenly! DON'T LEAN TO THE SIDE OR YOU'LL SPILL US!"

My arms ached and sweat stung my eyes. I was learning that the paddler in the rear—David—steered, and the paddler in the front—me—was merely a working passenger. We had arrived in Cooperstown with Mom and Dad the night before, and this day had been reserved for my canoeing lesson.

Sky and lake were the same gunmetal-blue color. The wind shifted to our backs, helping us glide across the surface as we paddled with easy, smooth strokes. I felt David's presence at the opposite end of the canoe; it reminded me of being on a teeter-totter, and I thought about the playground trick in which two people try to balance on one, with each rider in midair.

Mom and Dad watched from lawn chairs borrowed from our motel, which overlooked this tiny bay at the entrance to the Susquehanna. David and I slowly steered our canoe in a gentle ellipse and headed toward them. The head wind returned, stronger than before. Waves slapped the sides of the aluminum canoe, causing a faint metallic ring. I stroked harder.

"C'mon, paddle!" David yelled.

I shoveled water, and my chest burned. Waves spilled in and soaked my pants. David chopped the water and I struggled to match his rhythm. Clouds blotted out the sun; the sky and lake became gray.

"HARDER!" David shouted, and he splashed me with his paddle.

I yelped, spun around, and thus broke Canoeing Rule No. 1: No sudden weight shifts. The canoe flipped, and David and I plummeted into the water.

I choked on swallowed water and clawed my way to the surface. David bobbed beside me.

"You freaking idiot!" he shrieked as he clung to the swamped canoe.

I felt like a freaking idiot.

David swam for shore, arms flailing furiously. I gathered the floating paddles with one hand and pushed the swamped canoe with the other. With slow, steady kicks, I sliced through small concave waves, toward shore.

I beached the canoe and slumped down next to it. David had already reached shore and lay stretched on his back, gulping air. Water ran down my neck and dribbled past my heart.

Mom stood over David and made cooing sounds. Dad came directly to me and said in a hearty, cheerful voice, "You're one rotten canoeist!"

He clapped me on the shoulder, turned his head toward David, and laughed. "You two are going to have a helluva time!"

That was my entire canoe instruction. The next morning, Mom, David, and I sorted our camping gear. Mom carefully arranged the contents of my duffel bag, while David stuffed his absentmindedly. The door to our motel room opened and Dad entered, along with a damp early-morning breeze from Lake Otsego.

"Come and get it," Dad called. He removed a doughnut from a paper bag and handed it to Mom.

"Boston Creme. Your favorite," he said.

David and I got doughnuts, too.

"Coffee?" Mom asked.

"Coffee!" Dad replied, lifting a steaming paper cup from another bag. He handed her the cup and she smiled. Mom loved coffee. She would even avoid some restaurants because she knew they served bad coffee.

Dad handed David and me small bottles of orange juice. The four of us crowded on the end of the bed and ate. Mom raised her doughnut slightly and said, "Good."

"Yeah. I went to the little bakery a few doors down from the, uh, baseball place, uh, the Hall of Fame," he replied. Dad had never visited the Hall of Fame during his many visits to Cooperstown. He pronounced baseball "a bore and a half."

He looked at his doughnut and continued, "Not as good as Spiro's."

Spiro's was our local bakery.

"Remember David's graduation cake? That was something!" he said.

"And our anniversary cake. Chocolate mousse!" Mom added.

"Delicious!" Dad said. "Hey, let's get a special 'Welcome Home' cake from Spiro's."

"Gee, Dad, it's just a camping trip. It's not a big deal!" David noted.

"No, not the canoe trip. Vietnam. When you return from Vietnam. A 'Welcome Home' cake for that!" Dad said.

Mom sipped her coffee through frowning lips. Then she got up and continued packing my gear.

"I packed plenty of underwear and T-shirts, but only two pairs of blue jeans. I sewed the crotch and the knees on this one. They were coming apart. Why you didn't want a new pair is a mystery," she said.

Mom would never understand that a canoe trip was no place for stiff, unbroken-in jeans.

She continued packing: socks. Sneakers. An army-surplus rubberized poncho for the rain and to use as a ground cover under my sleeping bag. Three pairs of shorts cut from old blue jeans. They would do double duty as swimsuits, too. Mom wedged in a plastic box that held a toothbrush and soap. I added a flashlight, a small portable radio, and a paperback copy of the James Bond thriller *Goldfinger*. Besides our clothes, we were taking sleeping bags and a third duffle bag filled with aluminum cooking gear and food, mostly cereal and macaroni. There were several jars of peanut butter, too.

Dad opened a map of New York State.

"When the river leaves Cooperstown, it squiggles back and forth more than this road map shows. A lot more," he said as his finger traced the path of the Susquehanna. "Then it heads south, dips into Pennsylvania for a while, then curls into New York again for a bit before it swings back into Pennsylvania for the rest of the ride. It's really not much of a river until Pennsylvania. It's really wide in Harrisburg. You guys won't get that far. Way too far to go."

I could tell by his voice that he wanted to come with us. I wanted him to come, too.

"What about toilet paper?" Mom asked.

"We'll use leaves," David said, not looking up as he packed. Mom had tried to help him pack, but David's scowls had driven her away.

"We gotta wipe with *leaves*?" I asked.

"Nature's toilet paper!" Dad chuckled.

Mom made a sour face, dropped four rolls into a plastic bag, and pushed the bag into my duffel. Then she went to her suitcase, removed a small container, and marched to David's side. He looked up, and she lifted it to his eyes. He stared dumbly at the thick pink liquid.

"It's calamine lotion. Stops itching. For when you use poison ivy instead of toilet paper," she said, and she dropped the jar into his pack.

Dad burst out laughing, and I did, too. David was dark for a moment, but in the end he cracked up, too.

5

Not a single ripple disturbed Lake Otsego. The surface of the lake was an immense gray sheet pulled taut. *It's too perfect to disturb,* I thought to myself as I reluctantly reached down to launch the canoe. David must have felt the same way, because he hesitated, too.

"Let's go," he said in a low voice after a few moments.

We slid the loaded canoe into the lake and paddled a few yards to the entrance to the Susquehanna. We glided into the narrow stream and passed under a graceful footbridge where Mom and Dad stood. Dad sipped coffee and grinned broadly. Mom blew kisses. Then she wrapped her arms around herself, warding off a chill only she felt.

Dad waved and said, "Have fun, boys. Don't do anything stupid."

"And be careful," Mom called.

Dad took Mom's hand; their joined arms hung down like a slack rope.

Tall stiff trees splintered the early morning light. We slowly moved downstream. I looked back often and waved, until the river turned sharply and a row of evergreens blocked our view of Mom and Dad.

We heard Dad shout, "Look out for each other!"

Mom added an insistent "Love you! Be careful."

We yelled our good-byes and were on our own.

David said, "Let's try and make some miles. This part of the river sucks. I want to be done with it."

He might have added he wanted to be done with me, too. I could hear the resentment in his voice. I guess the thought of spending time with me bored him.

At first, David had been my great pal. But I was nearly five years younger than him, and eventually the time told. The things he had mastered, I was just learning. I couldn't play ball, build model airplanes, or fight the neighborhood bullies as well as he could. David didn't understand or want to understand. To him, I was a fumbling, weak *thing*. He started calling me "loser," "jerk," and "bozo." They were just silly words, but they hurt. Being my big brother eventually became an unpleasant chore, and the points where our lives touched had disappeared.

We paddled silently. The narrow river—a child could easily toss a rock across it—moved slowly, and scum coated its stagnant edges. Clouds of gnats hovered above the cola-colored water, and they made war on us when we pierced their swarms. The river snaked through woods. Fallen trees made crude dams, and we had to unload our equipment and haul the canoe over them. It was hard work, and soon I was slathered in sweat. A slip on a greasy wet log sent me crashing into the brush. Nettles scratched my arms and legs. David scowled at me and yanked the canoe clear by himself.

The river left the woods and wound through open meadows. The sun lay on us like a great weight. I felt soggy-headed and nauseous. My arms were heavy and I paddled slower. Even David's paddling faded, and the canoe barely moved. I stopped paddling completely. After a few more strokes, David stopped, too. A squadron of mosquitoes discovered us and started to feast. I feebly brushed them away. David finally drove them off with a splash of his paddle. He soaked me but I didn't care. I stared forward through half-closed eyes. *This is only the first day!* I thought, and I immediately felt even worse.

"Here," said David, and I felt his paddle poke me in the back.

Wearily, I turned around. A jar of peanut butter balanced on the blade of David's outstretched paddle. I quickly took it, unscrewed the top, and scooped out the creamy goop with my fingers. I licked them clean and ate another handful. I was about to take a third helping when I remembered David. I extended my arm and offered the jar, but he refused with a small shake of his head. I ate two more handfuls and passed the jar back to David. He stretched his legs over our equipment and made himself comfortable. Then he scooped out a large helping with two fingers and ate slowly.

"Man," he said, "I forgot how much canoeing sucks."

I blinked in surprise.

"I thought you liked canoeing," I replied. "You went with Dad all the time."

"*Dad* liked canoeing," David answered. "Paddling all day stinks. Man, I really hate sitting in a puddle of water all day. Camping on the river is fun. But not when there are bugs! Sometimes we'd be up all night with the freaking bugs! You know what was the best, the *best*? The drive to and from the river! We'd buy a loada crap—Ring Dings, Yodels—and stuff ourselves while we drove. We'd take leaks on the side of the road. We'd stop at greasy little diners and eat whatever. I could even have a hamburger and Coke for breakfast! And Dad would try to make the waitress if she was a real chick."

David eyed my surprise and sighed. "Ah, screw it."

After a long pause, he added, "Let's get over there. I gotta crap."

He pointed to a stand of birch trees at a bend in the river. We landed the canoe near the trees and pulled ashore. David scurried beyond the bank, dropped his pants, and squatted. I followed and hesitantly undid my pants as I looked around for unwanted spectators.

"What are you lookin' for?" asked David.

"What if somebody is watching?" I said.

He gazed at me blankly and then bent his frame so that his head was low and his bare bottom pointed skyward.

"Kiss my butt, world!" he screamed, then howled like a coyote. "Oooowwwwww! Oooowwww! Oowwwwwwwwww-www! Kiss my butt!"

After a moment, I dropped my pants and copied David's pose.

"Kiss my butt!" I shouted. "Kiss my butt, world! Oooo-wwww! Oowwwwwwwwwwww! "

We screamed and howled and howled and screamed until we were breathless and fell to the grass. "Kiss my butt," we yelled, laughing through gulps of air.

David hitched his pants and stood up. He scanned the horizon and measured the height of the sun.

"Let's get going. I want to get farther downriver before we pitch camp," David said. "I don't want to set up the tent in the dark."

I slowly zipped up my jeans as David returned to the canoe and muscled it back into the river. "Hurry up, loser," he yelled, "or I'll leave without you."

6

We spent the night on a ribbon of grass beside the river. I slept heavily and David had to shake me awake the next morning.

"I'm beat," I moaned.

"Eat this," David replied, pushing a cereal-filled canteen toward me.

He tossed me a spoon, then lay on his side and ate from his canteen. After we finished, he poured orange juice into the canteens. He slugged his portion down and then began to roll up his sleeping bag. I stared into my canteen. Bits of cereal floated in it. David hadn't waited for us to clean out the cups before adding the juice.

"Come on. Let's get cracking," he ordered, and I swallowed the juice in a long gulp.

We paddled until lunch, which was a meal of peanut butter and jelly sandwiches. Then more paddling, until the sun broiled and our arms and backs ached. We made a temporary camp, threw our sleeping bags on the ground, and napped. I arose stupid and groggy and dropped into the river to wake up. We climbed back into the canoe and traveled until dusk. We found a grassy landing where we decided to spend the night. David made a fire, and we ate a macaroni and cheese dinner. Darkness brought sleep.

Days followed with a dull sameness. I counted them: five days down, nine to go.

Although the river grew wider, it struck me more like a big stream. We paddled through small glades and pocket woodlands. There were signs of life—tractors, sheds, pickup trucks—but we didn't see many people. A narrow road drew near the river, and a tractor dragging an impossibly large load of hay slowly wheeled past. The driver saluted us and we responded with raised paddles. Still, it didn't spark excitement for either David or me; it was just a humdrum scene, a modest slice of rural America, for which neither of us had acquired a taste.

Mom would have loved it. Meandering back roads were her notion of heaven. Dad had other ideas, and more vigorous family activities were planned for him. We spent one Christmas in Canada learning to ski. Dad, despite his war injuries, picked it up quickly and attacked the toughest slopes. David learned quickly, too, and followed Dad down steep trails. They waited at the bottom of the hill while I came down gentler runs. Mom sat in the lodge and read. Still, she remembered the trip fondly. But when she recalled it she would say, "Remember the Canada vacation when we got lost and ended up at Loon Lake? And the cute restaurant, the one that was an antiques store, too?"

David and I paddled weakly and hardly spoke. I daydreamed. What were Scott, Terry, J. M., and Lip Man doing? We had been close friends since kindergarten and seemed never to be apart. During fourth grade, it was the sight of us walking five abreast, in height order, that prompted Linda LaTorrance to say we reminded her of the toes on a foot. A nickname was born, and we were the Toes ever after. I was Toe Number Four, the one next to the pinky. I wished I was with them.

Another snack of peanut butter on fingers broke the monotony. A bend in the river delivered a small grass-and-dirt landing, and David decided we should spend the night. We dragged the canoe ashore and unloaded. The sleeping bags were unfurled atop our rubberized ponchos. A cloudless sky offered little prospect of rain. David dug a fire pit, and I searched for twigs and branches within a stand of trees that formed a battlement around our site. I delivered the wood, and soon a healthy fire bloomed. David made a crude sawhorse from broken branches and hung a pot of canned spaghetti over the fire.

We threw ourselves on our sleeping bags and waited for dinner to heat up. We stared wordlessly at the frog-colored river that formed a horseshoe around us. On its far side was a grassy meadow that climbed to a low ridge that masked the world beyond. I fidgeted with clothes in my pack while David lay motionless. The spaghetti and the discomfort of our silence both slowly cooked.

"I'm going swimming," I finally announced.

I peeled off my T-shirt and shorts. As I ambled to the river's edge, David started laughing.

I looked at David quizzically. He pointed and giggled.

I looked down at my sticklike frame and saw my sunburned arms and legs. They were as red as strawberries and contrasted wildly with my vanilla-white trunk.

"You look like a candy cane!" David said through his guffaws.

It was a goofy thought and I started laughing, too.

"I think I'm gonna hang you from a Christmas tree!" David said, giggling. He got to his feet and raced toward me. I darted away, and the chase was on!

I raced away from our camp, along the river's edge, but David quickly caught up to me. I made tight curlicued paths ahead of him and just slipped his grasp. He fell and rolled on the muddy riverbank but was up again quickly. I skipped to and fro and high-stepped through calf-deep water, and David splashed doggedly after me. I lengthened my lead and padded into deeper water until the river bottom became loose and muddy. My feet sank into the gooey mess and I yelled, "It feels like I'm walking in snot!"

At that instant David tackled me, plunging the two of us underwater. As we somersaulted beneath the surface, David's grip failed; I popped up and gleefully crashed through deep water back toward the riverbank. Running and laughing, I was breathless.

David pounced on me again, but this time his arms pinned me as we sank. I swallowed water, choked, bucked and kicked, squirmed free, broke the surface and gasped, but only for an instant before David pulled me under again. Water sloshed down my throat and nose, and I clawed at David's tightly imprisoning arms. "Let go!" I shouted, but the words exploded into a million bubbles. My head roared with wordless panic; David was drowning me.

I felt myself being lifted from the water and tossed into the air. I inhaled hungrily before I tumbled back underwater. David was laughing as he grabbed me and tossed me again. I caught what little air I could. The drubbing made me light-headed.

On the fourth toss, I managed to shout, "Stop it! Stop!"

I hurtled through the air again. David snatched me from the water and lifted me over his head.

"I'm gonna hang this candy cane from a tree," he shouted with a laugh, and he carried me toward shore.

"STOP IT!" I screamed. I twisted free from his grasp and fell with a splash in front of him. I struggled to my feet and pushed David away with the last dregs of my strength. "STOP!"

David looked at me blankly.

"You almost drowned me, you jerk! You almost drowned me!"

I turned and rushed toward the riverbank.

"Don't be a baby!" David called after me.

I spun around and glared at David. I ached to hurt him but felt as powerless and helpless as a . . . baby. He stared back at me for a moment, shook his head slowly, and, with down-turned lips, trudged back toward the fire.

"Grow up," he mumbled as he brushed past me.

I was glad my wet face hid the tears running down my cheeks. Why did I feel stupid and small? David crouched next to the cook pot and studied its contents. The thought of joining him seemed like another defeat, so I remained anchored in ankle-deep water. My mind raced with ugly thoughts of hate and fear. I felt tired—exhausted, really—and not just from our fight. I was weary of his contempt.

I stood there for what seemed like forever until the wind came up, carrying the sweet, sticky stench of cow dung from the neighboring ridge. With it came a cloud of invisible bugs that surrounded me and chewed my neck, flanks, and limbs. Maddened by the attack, I galloped back to my clothes and threw them on. The bugs found David, and he danced in small circles, swatting wildly and futilely.

"Get the repellent," I shouted.

"I forgot it!" David yelped.

"But Mom told you—"

"Let's get outta here!"

He doused the fire with spaghetti sauce, then helped me scoop up our stuff, which we threw willy-nilly into the canoe. We launched ourselves onto the river, which was velvet-black in the light of a bright moon. We nosed the riverbank and looked for another campsite. We came upon a likely spot but were quickly driven away by a renewed bug attack. Eventually we found a small ribbon of grass beside the river where there were no bugs and little smell.

We landed the canoe, and I was starting to unpack when

David said, "Just pull out the sleeping bags and forget the rest. It's too late to make camp."

When we spread the bags, I discovered that mine had gotten wet during our hasty retreat.

"Use my bag," David grunted.

When I protested, he growled, "Just take it."

It was his way of apologizing. I just wasn't certain if it was for picking a crummy campsite or for half drowning me.

7

David awoke the next morning cursing the damp sleeping bag. His grumpiness worsened when we discovered that many of our clothes were wet as well.

"What are we going to do?" I asked. "Spread everything on the ground?"

"I'm not gonna waste half the day waiting for the sun to dry all this stuff," he said, and he angrily stuffed the wet items into one pack. He collected the rest of our gear and tossed it all, including our food pack, into the canoe. There would be no breakfast this morning.

We launched the canoe and sliced the thin, cottony mist covering the river. The low, early sun threw dramatic shadows across everything. The air cradled a tangy scent of fresh-turned earth, cut grass, and clear water. As the sun rose, the mist disappeared and the greens of the trees and grass became richer. David was silent and scowling.

A town appeared. It wasn't like the sad, shabby, back-road affairs we had passed before; this was a real village, with traffic lights, gas stations, a supermarket, a post office, and all kinds of shops. Best of all, at least for David and me, it had a Laundromat.

"We can dry our stuff there," David murmured, his mood appearing to brighten.

The trees and brush that normally lined the river gave way to cottages and other modest houses. We landed the canoe in the backyard of one of them—a tiny wheat-colored house with a red roof. Tall orange day lilies grew in patches along the river, and a thick stand of black-eyed Susans bordered the back of the house. I had helped Mom plant the same kinds of flowers in our garden. A long gravel driveway led to the town's main street. A brown car with a dull finish was parked in the driveway.

"Let's see if we can leave our stuff here while we head into town," David said.

As we pulled the canoe clear of the water, a border collie surprised us. She surveyed our gear with a wagging tail, then trotted up to me, stood with her front paws on my chest, and licked my face. I gently stroked her head until she eased herself down.

"Pepper, leave those boys alone," ordered an elderly woman from the back door of the house. Pepper sprinted away and raced indoors. The woman waved to us, smiled, and disappeared inside the house.

"Can you imagine the kind of greeting Venom would have given us?" David asked.

Venom was Ol' Lady Venman, Scott Venman's grand-mother. Scott was a neighbor and fellow Toe, and his grand-mother lived nearby. Grandma Venman hated everyone, including grandson Scott, and spent her waking hours rudely lecturing passers-by from her front window. Visitors like mail carriers and meter readers received special, height-ened insults. Trespassing children, especially grandson Scott, ignited explosions of rage that frightened us all, except Scott, who responded by gulping air and belching at her.

The gentleness of Pepper's owner was a startling contrast to Venom, the only old person David and I really knew. None of our grandparents were alive, and few old people lived in our neighborhood. Eighty-three-year-old Mrs. Mills lived in a house at the end of our street, but she was feeble and housebound and we rarely saw her. A gray-haired black woman cared for her and was as rarely seen as Mrs. Mills. No one knew the caretaker's name; she was always referred to as "the nice colored lady from the Mills house." In contrast to the few old people like Venom and Mrs. Mills, the neighbor-hood was brimming with kids, virtually all of whom were the children of parents from the World War II generation. All us boys wanted to be like our dads, and we endlessly refought the D-day, Wake Island, and Guadalcanal battles in their honor. Mom didn't like our war games; she quietly con-fiscated our toy guns, but they were quickly replaced and she finally gave up.

We carried the wet sleeping bag and clothes past the old woman's house. We could see her through the screened back door. She was chopping vegetables with gusto while glancing at a small TV that was perched on her kitchen counter. Her eyes were bright and her plain sleeveless dress revealed well-muscled arms. Pepper pressed against the wire screen, which made a waffle pattern on her nose.

The woman saw us and chirped in a high, strong voice, "Don't mind Pepper. She's just a darn friendly one. And don't worry about your things. They're safe—Pepper and I'll keep our eyes on them. Have yourselves a nice day and come back when you're ready. Just let me know if you'll be camping the night. I'll keep Pepper indoors if you are. We can't have Pepper sharing your sleeping bag with you."

Her unadorned generosity utterly charmed me.

"Yes, ma'am. Thanks, ma'am. Don't worry about Pepper, we like dogs. Have a wonderful day, ma'am," I called while transmitting my best 100-watt grin.

When we were several paces away, David giggled, "*Yes, ma'am, thanks, ma'am, have a wonderful day, ma'am.* What are you, the ambassador from planet Brown Nose?"

"Hey, I was trying to be nice," I replied.

"Have a wonderful day!" He laughed.

He was mocking me, but good-naturedly—the way you do with buddies, pals, guys-you-hang-with. It made me feel special.

"*Have a wonderful day!*" he repeated in a squeaky falsetto voice. "*Yes, ma'am, thanks, ma'am.*"

We started laughing and didn't stop until our cries drained us of our strength and we staggered over the driveway gravel weeping, hunched over like old men. Weak with delight, David dropped the wet sleeping bag to the ground. We fell on top of it and began to laugh more.

"Who are you, President Fumbler of the United States of Dorks?" I howled, and I collapsed next to him.

The ruckus set Pepper to barking and suddenly she appeared. The dog fell on us, licking the tears of laughter off our faces. Moments later, the old woman tiptoed hesitantly down the driveway. She watched for a moment, then chuckled.

"Come on in the house, Pepper," she called with a clap of the hands as she headed back to her kitchen. "Those boys are sick with the sillies and I don't want you comin' down!"

Pepper vaulted over me and raced away.

David and I happily moaned. We rolled onto our backs and stared up at the sky through the fingerlike leaves of an overhanging willow tree. The light from a bright sun filtered unevenly through the leaves and made odd-shaped shadows, like paint splattered on a wall. The dewy, warm air swaddled us. Everything was hushed, save for the slightest murmur of swaying leaves.

"Man, I could use a beer," David said.

"Yeah, me too," I replied.

David quickly sat up, stared at me, and began stammering, "Beer...what...why, you better not...drinking beer, 'cause..."

I quickly said, "Hello. Nice to make your acquaintance. I'm Professor Gotcha from Fooled U. *Have a wonderful day!*"

David's expression clouded, but just for a moment. Then

he brightened and exploded with laughter. His giant guffaws eventually shrank to happy moans. He looked at me, licked the tip of his finger, and chalked one up for me on an invisible scoreboard in the air.

"One point, little Stevie," he announced.

I loved it, and a goofy grin stretched across my face, though I wasn't thrilled with the "little" title.

"Come on, let's get this stuff dried," he said. He stood up and reached his hand out. I took hold, and he pulled me up.

8

As our clothes dried, I curled up in one of the Laundromat's bubblegum-pink plastic chairs. The spinning washing machines and tumbling dryers made a humming, mechanical lullaby that made me sleepy. David sat beside me and read a discarded newspaper. We didn't notice the two girls until they were standing in front of us.

Judging by their round hips and chests, I guessed they were eighteen years old. Their long, dark, straight hair fell to the middle of their backs. Their arms looked muscular, and neither appeared to be a stranger to hard work. Were they farm girls? One wore a brightly colored tie-dyed T-shirt; the other, a scruffy blue work shirt with an American flag embroidered on the front. Their blue jeans were tattered and had bell-bottoms.

"Do you have change?" one of the girls asked, a dollar bill in one hand and a laundry bag in the other. "The change machine is broken."

"Uh, sure," David said. He fumbled in his pocket and produced four quarters.

They put their clothes in a washer, glancing at David often and smiling. After a few moments, he joined them. I wasn't surprised by his boldness. David had had several girlfriends. I stayed in my chair; girls frightened me. The trio chatted. I didn't have to hear them; their body language was unmistakable. Introductions were made. David pointed to me; I could almost lip-read "little brother." He waved his hand toward the river and the girls' faces lit up with excitement about our adventure. Then their expressions turned sober and concerned. I guessed David was explaining he was a soldier and was going to Vietnam. A moment later, David walked back to me.

"Just don't be a jerk, OK?" he whispered as soon as he got close. "They're coming back to the canoe with us. They're high school seniors. I told them you were sixteen. Act it!"

David introduced me to Nina and Libby. I said hello but was stumped for anything else to say. I was relieved when David made small talk with them as we all waited for our clothes to wash. The girls told us they had been friends since kindergarten and planned to go to community college together and study nursing.

"Steve is going to be a doctor," David lied. He knew I wanted to be an architect. "Right, Steve?"

Nina and Libby giggled and said something about our maybe working together someday. I didn't know what to answer, and I just stood there with my mouth half open. Then

David lied that I had become a first aid expert for our trip and how safe it made him feel during our dangerous trip.

I wasn't sure if he was trying to impress the girls or see me squirm, but I was glad when he turned the conversation to our journey. When he told them where we had landed our canoe, Libby clapped her hands and laughed. "Oh my God, you're at Aunt Ginny's!"

We learned that Aunt Ginny was her grandmother's sister. Libby also said that she owned one of Pepper's puppies, named Spicer.

Libby and Nina offered to head back to Aunt Ginny's with us after our wash was done. David loved the idea. I nodded in agreement, but I was unsure. Was David going to put me on the spot again?

Soon the four of us set out, the girls beside David and me trailing. When we reached Aunt Ginny's, her brown car wasn't in the driveway.

"Must be at Grandma's," Libby said. "They spend alotta time together."

The girls suddenly raced for the canoe. David started to chase after them, then stopped and wrapped his arm around my neck.

"Hang in there, doc." He laughed, squeezing me. Then he raced away.

I just walked. By the time I reached the others, they had already dragged the canoe partway into the river. I steadied the canoe as the three of them piled in.

"Let 'er rip!" David yelled.

I shoved the canoe forward, and the girls shrieked and laughed. David paddled upstream and curved to the river's far side. Nina splashed Libby, and the two giggled. David's paddling slackened; he stroked just hard enough to hold the canoe motionless against the current. Libby dangled one foot in the water and rested the other on David's thigh. The three smiled and talked, but they were too far away for me to hear.

I was glad I was on shore and didn't have to pretend to be sixteen. I lay down on the grass. The afternoon sun beat down and a faint breeze carried the delicate perfume of Aunt Ginny's flower garden. A dragonfly hovered over the water. The crackle of tires rolling over gravel awakened me from my daydreams. The brown car came up the driveway and stopped. Aunt Ginny emerged, waved, and walked toward me. Pepper vaulted from the car, raced to the the riverbank, and barked at the canoe.

"Aunt Ginny! Aunt Ginny!" called Libby from the river. She and Nina waved madly.

"Libby? Hi, sweetheart!" she called.

David paddled back to shore. I waded into the river and helped the girls from the canoe.

"Thanks," Nina said as she stepped onto shore, gripping my shoulder for balance. Her hair brushed my face. It smelled like cut grass and lemons. Libby left the canoe next, ran to her great-aunt, and hugged her.

"Libby darling, do you know these boys?" Aunt Ginny said.

"New friends. We were hoping to make a picnic," she replied.

Aunt Ginny sized David and me up, then said, "OK, but you'll have to pitch in with the cooking. And cleaning! Understood? I'm not doing all the work. I'll call your mothers and tell them you're with me."

We spent the next hour in Aunt Ginny's kitchen. I helped make the hamburger patties and cut lettuce and vegetables for the salad. Aunt Ginny and Nina talked. Despite their difference in age, they chatted easily about the new gymnasium at the high school, vegetable gardens, Bill Vicker's noisy truck, and did-anyone-want-a-cat-cuz-the-Munders'-calico-had-kittens? David and Libby volunteered to set the picnic table.

The sun cast long shadows as we squeezed ourselves around Aunt Ginny's small redwood picnic table. Aunt Ginny asked David and me about our family and our canoe trip. When David told her about Vietnam, her face softened and she touched him on the forearm.

"You be careful over there. Three boys from our county have been there. Robbie Edwards, he was a pilot. Navy, I think. Works for Pan American Air Lines now. Ernie Shelby. He's career military. And Tommy Cuddleston. Buddy and Ethel's boy. He was only nineteen," she said, and then sighed. "Well, enough about *that*!"

We finished dinner. Aunt Ginny swept the bits of uneaten food from our plates into a bowl and slid them under the table, where Pepper waited.

"I have a treat for us," she announced, and she disappeared into the kitchen.

Libby glanced toward the house to make sure Aunt Ginny

was gone, then leaned her head forward and said in a low, conspiratorial voice, "Nina scored."

Nina reached into her front pocket and removed a bit of tinfoil that was smaller than a gum wrapper. She unwrapped it and revealed a squashed, brown-black *thing* that was about the size of a pencil eraser. As she slid her hand forward to give us a better look, she glanced backward and checked again for Aunt Ginny.

"Hash. Thai hash," Libby said. "Do you guys want to get high?"

The two girls smiled expectantly. I didn't know what to say; the only person I knew who got high was Robbie Lewis, a friend of David's. He smoked pot and went to the University of Pennsylvania. Had David tried it?

"We have a great place to get stoned," Nina added. "It's an abandoned farmhouse. The people left and—"

"All their stuff is still there. Beds. Chairs. A butter churn..." Libby added.

"There's even one of those old record players. Oh, what's it called? A vil, a vit, a—"

"Victrola," I offered.

"Yeah, that's it! Please come. We'll have a riot!"

"I..." I fumbled for words.

"*We*..." David said, with a hint of anger in his voice.

"Vanilla ice cream and baked apples!" called Aunt Ginny as she emerged from the house, carrying a large tray.

"Shhh," Libby whispered, and Nina quickly folded the tinfoil and stuffed it into her pocket.

"This is Libby's favorite!" the old woman exclaimed as she set the tray down. "Her last birthday, she insisted on baked apples and ice cream instead of cake. Isn't that true, dear?"

"Cake isn't as good!" Libby said.

"Yes, but do you know how hard it was to get fourteen candles to stand up in a mushy baked apple?" asked Aunt Ginny.

David's eyes widened and he gazed at Libby. She and Nina reddened and kept their eyes lowered on the dessert. It took me a moment to understand: Libby was only fourteen! Nina probably was, too!

After we finished dessert, the girls helped gather the dishes and carry them into the kitchen. When they were out of earshot, I said, "I thought you said they—"

"They told me they were seniors," David interrupted.

"*I'm* fourteen!"

"I know that! Listen, I'm going to tell them that we have to get going at dawn and we gotta go to sleep early. That we can't hang out. Play along. Man, what a dope I am. Can't spot a *fourteen-year-old*!"

Libby and Nina left shortly after dinner. There was no more talk of getting high or explanations about their true age. They simply said good night and went home. Later that evening, David and I lay in our sleeping bags beside Aunt Ginny's flower bed. Pepper appeared out of the darkness and lay down between us. I stroked her flank. The low drone of Aunt Ginny's TV carried on the evening air to us. I thought

David would say something about the hash, but instead he asked, "The girls were funny, huh?"

"Yeah," I said.

"Fourteen! God!"

After a moment of silence, David began to giggle.

"Doctor Steve," he chuckled. "You should have seen your face. Like you'd crapped your pants! I thought you'd pick up on what I was doing. I was gonna crack up."

"You were messing with *them*?"

"What, you thought I was messing with *you*? Why would I do that?"

"I dunno."

"You must think I'm a real loser." David laughed. "Well, it doesn't make a difference anyway, because in the end they messed with *us*!"

We laughed, disturbing Pepper, who stood for a moment before settling back down to her original position.

"Doctor Steve," David murmured as he rolled over and went to sleep.

9

David began calling me Doctor Steve all the time. At first it was funny, but after two days I finally snapped, "Enough! Just drop it!"

"What's eating you?" he barked. "Bozo."

I hated being called "bozo," "jerk," or "loser," or any of the other nasty titles he flipped my way. But I had lost that battle with him many years ago, and I didn't say anything.

We paddled in silence.

The river had grown as wide as a highway. Dense scrub brush covered its banks like a ruffle. The pull of the current strengthened, and David and I were content to drift with only our modest assistance. Pastures covered in corn stalks or clover slid past. A town appeared, arriving and disappearing with peekaboo swiftness. The sun rose, and its heat covered me like a shroud.

My mind wandered. What were the Toes up to? They were

probably in Scott's basement. It was like a clubhouse to us. There were sofas and easy chairs, but they were old and his mom never cared if we spilled food on them. There was a big TV and an old refrigerator filled with snacks.

"Not me," Scott had said when I told him about the canoe trip with David. "Two weeks alone with Ken and I'd end up dead." Ken was his older brother and David's buddy. Scott and Ken fought, really fought, with punches and kicks. Scott's arm was broken during one fight.

"*I* should go with David," Scott added. Scott got on well with David, better than I did. But then, Ken liked me better than he liked Scott.

"You still hot for Linda what's-her-name? LaTorrance?" David asked, breaking the silence and surprising me with his knowledge of a personal secret. Linda and I had known each other since we were infants. Mom even had a picture of us sharing a baby bath. I hated it when Mom showed it to her friends.

"Yeah, I guess," I mumbled.

"Does she like you?"

"I think she likes Lip Man."

"The *dancer*?"

Lip Man took dance lessons instead of playing sports, and lot of guys razzed him. But not too much; Lip Man never walked away from a fight.

"Screw him. You should ask her out." David said.

"I guess."

"Ask her out. Don't be a jerk," he said, and he lifted his

paddle from the river. "I'm bushed. Let's quit for the day."

A bend in the river revealed a grassy campus with large, well-kept buildings with freshly painted facades, but a peek through their windows revealed gutted, ghostly interiors. There was no clue about what the buildings once housed or why they had been abandoned. It was eerie.

"I'm not spending the night there," David said, echoing my thoughts. We glided past.

We traveled another hour, until we reached a sandy landing beside a small railroad bridge, and beached the canoe. Judging from the rust on the rails, they hadn't been used in a long time. The old railway, and a dirt tractor path beside it, divided a large weedy pasture from a thick woods. At the end of the field was a narrow country road. We made camp, then hiked the tractor path to the road in hopes of spying a nearby town. Our hunch was rewarded when we spotted a village about a mile away. We set off for it, in no great hurry. After passing rows and rows of corn, we reached a crossroads with a gas station, a feed store, and a general store. We explored the general store, treading on its unpainted, unwaxed wooden floor and searching its thinly stocked shelves. While we shopped, a skinny, white-haired, sour-faced clerk silently watched us. He seemed relieved when we left after purchasing soft drinks, Slim Jims, and cookies. We snacked quietly on the steps of the store. I watched a couple of sparrows land in a puddle of water and bathe. They leaped into the air when David stood, stretched, and said, "Let's head back."

At dusk, we arrived at the dirt path that led to our camp.

Halfway down it, David stopped and stared into the woods.

"What's—" I said before he hushed me with a quickly upraised hand.

He looked into the blackness for several moments.

"Come on, let's get—"

Before I finished, he clamped one hand behind my neck and the other over my mouth, and pulled me down into a crouch. He put his lips against my ear and whispered, "There is something in the woods."

Geez, this is a cheap trick! I thought, shaking off David's hands so I could tell him so. But he pressed harder and repeated, "There is something in the woods!"

His eyes pleaded with me until I relaxed.

He released me, commanded me to silence with his finger over pursed lips, then pulled me over the tracks and into the woods.

We stood in the embrace of a tall bush. David stared into the forest. I tried to follow his gaze but couldn't see anything except the odd shadows made from the light of a rising moon over the trees. When his attention returned to me, my eyes revealed my puzzlement. He slowly lifted his arm and pointed into the heart of the woods. At that moment, I noticed something yellow and glimmering rising faintly from the forest floor. It was the light from a fire, low and steady and anchored to that one spot: a campfire.

David gestured with the palm of his hand for me to hold still. Then he slipped into the brush, toward the fire. His absence unnerved me. The whispering sounds of the night rumbled in my head. I trembled at the touch of a breeze. *Rabbits must feel this way,* I thought to myself. *How can they stand it?*

I was grateful when David emerged from the gloom. But my relief was short-lived. With a tilt of his head, David directed me to follow him back into the brush. Reluctantly I plodded after him through bushes and trees. Every few steps, David froze and I did, too; the two of us were as motionless as wary deer. Every snapped twig, every airborne scent, each murmur of the night became stark and vivid.

We halted by a wide evergreen. David peeked his head around the tree for an instant, then ducked back. He edged away and pulled me beside him. It was my turn to spy, and I tilted my head into position.

A small fire of stubby logs was burning in a shallow pit at the center of a sloppy campsite. Clothes hung on a line strung between two trees. Two battered backpacks, open and spilling clothes, lay beside a tattered sleeping bag. Two pans and a pot were overturned near the fire. An empty soup can rested half in the flames.

But no one was there.

I turned and looked back at David. He lifted his eyebrows in puzzlement. He signaled me to follow him, and we slipped back through the brush to the railroad tracks.

"Why would somebody leave a campsite like that, with the fire going and all?" I quietly asked.

"I dunno. It's really weird," answered David.

"What bugs me is that our campsite is so close by," he

continued. "I don't want some weirdo sneakin' up on us in the middle of the night."

Then, with a start, he stiffened. "Damn! Damn, damn!"

"What's wrong?" I asked.

"All our stuff. It's close by—and nobody's watching it!" he replied, and he set off in a dog trot toward our site. I followed, a few steps behind.

We were there in moments. We paused briefly at the tree line to assure ourselves that no one else was about. Then David darted around the site, pushing his hands inside the packs, looking, taking inventory. I watched, but my nervousness kept my attention directed on the black woods.

"Everything seems to be here," he said, his voice trailing off. "But..."

"But what?" I asked.

"Did we leave that there?" he asked, pointing to our food pack. "And did we leave our packs open?"

I couldn't remember. But I understood his point: someone had rifled through our things.

"Let's get outta here," I said.

"I'm not gonna let some creep chase me away!" David answered sharply. "No way!"

"Having a maniac for a neighbor isn't the best thing for a good night's sleep," I complained.

David scowled. "Yeah, but I'm still not running away! Grab one sleeping bag," he ordered, then went to his pack and removed something from deep within it.

"C'mon," he said, and he moved swiftly in a crouch along

the riverbank. I hunched over and ran close behind him. We stopped about thirty yards downstream.

"Let the creep think we're still over there while we sleep here," said David. "We're close to the water so no one can sneak up behind us, and there's the field in front so we'll be able to spot anybody coming. Unzip the bag. It'll be big enough for the two of us to lie on. It's warm out, so we won't need a cover. We'll sleep in shifts. I'll take the first lookout."

With that, he revealed the item he had removed from his pack: a large folding buck knife. He opened it and stabbed the gleaming four-inch blade into the sod. He kept his hand tightly wrapped around the handle and stared into the night.

I lay on my side and stared at the knife until I fell asleep.

I awoke to the low, ceaseless hum of millions of noisily employed insects. The night was black; morning was still far off. I propped myself up on one arm. David turned to me for an instant, then quickly looked away. He was still holding the buck knife.

"Hey, let me be lookout. It's my turn," I whispered.

"I got it. Go back to sleep," he answered.

"Come on, David. I can do it. If you don't get any sleep, you'll be miserable tomorrow."

After a few moments, he grudgingly said OK.

"Don't fall asleep!" he growled, "I'm counting on you. And hold onto this." He raised the knife and thrust it into the ground in front of me. I placed my fingers around the handle, which was still damp and warm from David's hand. He rolled onto his side and, using his bent arm as a pillow, faced me. I felt his eyes gauging me, not trusting me to stay awake. I stared straight ahead for a long time before I glanced back to see if he was still watching, still judging.

Our eyes met.

"I got it covered!" I said through gritted teeth.

He looked at me for a moment, then slowly rolled over.

When I was sure he had fallen asleep, I released the buck knife; holding it made me feel silly. I wasn't afraid anyway. I could see no one was sneaking up on us. In fact, I could see nearly everything—the fields, the river, the railroad bridge— all painted in shades of dark purple. I watched a raccoon emerge from the brush, waddle to the river, slip into the water, and swim away. Two bats flew out of the trees and flitted back and forth across the sky. I heard the scurry of small feet but never saw their owner. Something large and dark glided above me, its wings riding the current of a barely felt breeze—an owl? The night cast a spell that kept me alert until dawn, when David awoke with a start. He scooped up the buck knife, folded it, slipped it into his pocket, and hopped to his feet.

"Come on," he said, and he started back toward our original camp.

David made a quick accounting of our gear, and then he plunged into the woods. I hesitated for a moment, but the prospect of waiting alone was scarier than entering the gloomy woods, so I trotted after him. He crashed through the brush. I caught up to David just as he reached the site of the mysterious camp.

It was empty. The only evidence of its existence was some crushed boughs where the sleeping bag had rested and the soggy ashes of a drowned campfire.

"Creepy," David said.

"Too creepy for me. Let's get outta here," I said, backing away.

"*Really* creepy," he said.

"Let's go!" I screamed, and I plunged into the brush. I didn't wait for David. I was nearly through the woods when I heard something crashing after me. I froze and my heart leaped into my mouth. David raced past me.

"Run!" he shouted.

I leaped after him.

"Run!" he called. "It's the bogeyman!"

When I emerged from the woods, I saw David laughing.

"You afraid of the bogeyman?" he said.

"You jerk. Why'd you do that?" I barked.

"Come on. It was just a joke."

I fumed.

"Come on. It was just a joke," he repeated.

I didn't say anything.

"I wasn't trying to really scare you," David pleaded.

I stayed silent, and David said, "I'm sorry."

"Don't do it again!" I said angrily. "And what were you planning to do if somebody had been at that camp?"

"I don't know," he said chuckling. "I just figured we could

surprise him and give him a scare. I didn't really think it through."

"I thought you had a plan," I said.

"Nope."

I stared at him.

"Geez, you give me a lot more credit than I deserve." He laughed and began to load our gear into the canoe.

10

"What about breakfast?" I asked as we launched the canoe.

"We're out," he said. "We need milk and cereal. Water. Alotta stuff. We gotta find a grocery."

David dug a jar of peanut butter from a pack and held it up to me. I shook my head. I was sick of peanut butter. A short while later, we passed a house and got permission to refill our canteens from a spigot. We hoped to find food as easily, but didn't. Three times we passed roads, and each time we beached the canoe and unsuccessfully searched for a store.

It was nearly noon when we came to a narrow bridge. We nosed the canoe into the riverbank, and I waited while David scrambled to the road. I was bored and hungry. My mind was blank, and David startled me when he screamed, "Stevie! Get up here! Quick!"

I remembered David's earlier bogeyman trick and yelled, "Cut it out, David!"

"Get up here. Really!" he called.

"This better be good!" I hollered. I climbed out of the canoe and pulled it ashore. I scurried up the weedy embankment and met David, who was staring down the road. About a hundred yards away was a Dairy Queen ice cream stand.

"What's that doing in the middle of nowhere?" I asked.

"I don't care!" he shouted, and he sprinted toward it.

I raced after him and arrived at the stand just a step behind him. We sidled up to its window but no one was there. Voices trailed from the back of the store.

"Hello," David called. "Anyone there?"

A blond-haired woman with a red apron and a bright smile appeared from behind a partition.

"Sorry. Didn't hear you pull up," the woman explained.

She wiped her hands with a pink flowered cloth and looked past us into the empty parking lot.

"No car? Where did you boys come from?" she asked.

"The river," I said. "We're canoeing it."

"Really?" she replied, and she turned toward the back of the store. "Dad, come here. There are some boys you should talk to."

A thin bald man ambled from behind the partition. His red Dairy Queen polo shirt hung on him like a dishrag on a hook.

"And why would I want to speak with some boys?" he asked in a gentle voice.

"They're canoeing the river," she answered.

The man straightened and moved to the window. The

woman stepped aside so that he could stand in front of David and me.

"I canoed it in '38. Well, most of it. From here to Havre de Grace," he said.

"Our dad went the whole way," David offered.

"I like the man already," he replied.

"He says it builds men," David joked, shooting me a side-long glance.

"Yes it does!" the man agreed earnestly.

"Dad canoed the river several times. And you took Tom and Matthew that time," the woman added.

"Took my sons in 'fifty-three," the man exclaimed. "They hated it."

"No they didn't. They still talk about it," she protested good-naturedly.

"Talk about how much they hated it," he replied, smiling, and the woman laughed.

"*I* would have enjoyed it," she offered, brushing long bangs from her eyes.

"Achhh, you're a girl. What sense is there in taking a girl on a camping trip, Olivia?"

"You can tell my dad is from the old school," Olivia said to David and me. "There's no room for women in the woods."

"Don't start with that women's lib stuff with me!" the man replied.

"You want me burn my bra, Dad?" she chided him.

"Achhh!"

There were broad smiles on both of their faces. It seemed

to me that their argument about women's rights had long ago turned into a familiar, family comedy act.

The old man told us his river adventures, gentle tales about flipping the canoe and sleeping in pigpens. He told us of dangers to avoid in Maryland. I didn't have the heart to tell him we wouldn't be traveling that far. I guess David felt the same way, because he didn't say anything either.

The old man started to tell us about his navy career in World War II.

"Didn't have to enlist. I was already married. Had my two boys already. Never would have had to serve," he said.

"Dad, take a breath!" Olivia interrupted. "And let these boys order some ice cream," she chuckled.

"Oh. Yes. Of course. Didn't mean to bore you. Ice cream. What'll you have?" the man said.

"You didn't bore us," David answered. "Can I have a black-'n'-white shake?"

I ordered an upside-down banana split. We sat at an ancient picnic table beside the shop and ate, basking in the unusually warm sun. Above us, a hawk made figure eights as it looked for its breakfast.

Terry Hudson, one of the Toes, knew everything about hawks. Hawks and owls were his favorite birds, and he had a shelf full of books about them. One winter Terry convinced me to rise at dawn and head to the beach in hopes of sighting a rare snowy owl. And we did, too, and spotted the bird, as white as an angel, as it rose from the dunes and soared over our heads. I wished Terry was with me on the river.

"C'mon, let's head back to the canoe," David said, interrupting my thoughts and snatching up my unfinished ice cream.

"Hey! I'm not finished," I bawled as he dropped his empty shake and my ice cream into a garbage can.

"You've been staring at it, not eating, for ten minutes," he answered. "Looked like you were done to me. It's time to get going, anyway."

"Get me another one," I argued. He was holding all our money.

"Yeah, right," he replied in a voice thick with sarcasm.

I stood there for a moment as he walked away.

"You're a real freaking idiot!" I shouted.

He just kept walking.

I chased after him.

"Give me money for another ice cream," I screamed, grabbing for his pocket. He wrestled me away and shoved me to the ground. I was about to leap up and go at him again when a shiny new Ford sedan appeared from behind the Dairy Queen. Olivia was driving it and rolled to a halt beside us.

"I'm running errands. Need a lift?" she asked, eyeing me oddly for a moment.

David quickly agreed and hopped into the front. I arose slowly, dusted myself off, and slid into the rear seat, still fuming.

Olivia turned to look at me and asked, "Are you OK?"

I nodded my head weakly, and she pulled away.

Before we had left the parking lot, David asked, "Do you know if there is a grocery store nearby?"

"There's a big chain supermarket in town. That would do, wouldn't it?" she said.

We discovered that the ice cream stand was on the fringe of a bustling town. Olivia parked at a large food store and said, "Go get your groceries and I'll take you back to the river."

We protested that she needn't wait for us, that she had already been generous in driving us to the market, but she ignored us. When David and I emerged from the market with three bags of groceries, she was waiting, smiling.

11

Later, the afternoon sun became scalding. After a couple of hours paddling beneath it, I said, "We should have stayed at the Dairy Queen."

David grunted weakly.

The air felt soggy and the trees and brush drooped. The water was flat and appeared motionless; scum accumulated on the riverbank like cobwebs on an unused window. My mouth was dry and cottony, and I thought about how nice it would be to suck an ice cube. I unpacked a carton of orange juice and drank. It had been cold when we bought it but now it was lukewarm. My thoughts kept me from noticing that David had stopped paddling. I turned to him and saw he was staring up at the sky. A boiling thunderhead towered above us like a monster.

"I don't want to be out in the open when this storm hits," David said.

We searched the thickly wooded riverbank for an opening, but there was heavy brush everywhere. The river twisted to the right and back to the left. We passed beneath a weeping willow, and its overhanging branches made a curtain that hung to the water and tore at our arms as we paddled.

A deer exploded out of the nettles and crashed into the water in front of us.

"Geez!" David shouted, and he spun the canoe. I reeled and nearly lost my paddle.

The deer passed so close that I could have reached out and stroked it. We watched it swim to the far bank, wiggle into the brush, and disappear. Was it trying to escape the storm, too?

The wind stiffened and swirled, carrying bits of bark, dirt, and twigs. Small choppy waves churned the river. The canoe skidded to and fro as if stung by the electricity of the rising storm.

"There," David barked, his eyes fixed on some kind of shelter on a rise above the water.

We paddled hard. The storm clouds blackened and spread as if racing us to shore. Windblown trees and bushes swayed madly. Thunder rumbled. I felt it in my stomach.

"Come on! Come on!" I shouted.

We drove the nose of the canoe directly onto the bank. I leaped out, stumbled, and fell flat. David muscled me to my feet by the back of my pants and shirt. For an instant, everything became stark white. Thunder cracked; it sounded like something immense snapping.

Twenty yards away on a bluff above the river there stood a rough shelter—just a long roof supported by crude beams sunk in the dirt. We raced to it. We were within three strides of the shelter when the wind and rain blasted us. We skidded into the shelter, already soaked and dripping. Torrents of water cascaded off the roof and made muddy pools that quickly spread to our feet.

In the shelter were two rows of wooden picnic tables. David hopped onto one and sat down. I climbed onto another and drew my knees to my chest. Lightning struck nearby and I heard the drawn-out crash of a tree falling.

The heavy rain made a gray veil. I slid off the table and went to check on the canoe.

"Get back!" David yelled.

I jumped at his harshness but remained at the edge of the shelter.

He looked at me and then repeated, more softly, "Get back. It's safer. The lightning and all."

I retreated slowly back to the table.

"Three guys from my company at Fort Dix were killed by lightning," David explained. "We were on the parade ground when a storm hit. The drill instructor ordered everyone into the barracks. We raced like hell. Except these guys. They lagged behind and...just stay back, OK?"

"They got blasted?" I asked.

David nodded.

"Did you tell Mom and Dad?"

"Are you nuts? It would have made Mom crazy."

David was right. "Be careful!" punctuated nearly every sentence Mom uttered to us. But we never listened, and we regularly shredded our shins, thumped our skulls, and unhinged our teeth. Of course, Mom didn't get any help from Dad.

When I was six, he introduced David to Blind Man Biking. Dad would pedal with his eyes shut while David perched on the handlebars and shouted directions. I stood at the curb and watched them turn wobbly circles and fractured figure eights. They bounced into parked cars and bumped over the curb. When they crashed, they'd roll on the ground, giggling.

"You won't be laughing when someone gets hurt," said Mom when she discovered the game.

Once, when Dad wasn't available, David convinced me to try Blind Man Biking. He mounted his bike and I climbed onto the handlebars, facing forward, my legs straddling the front wheel. David pushed us forward and started pedaling.

"I'm shutting my eyes!" David shouted.

We rolled straight for a moment, then swerved back and forth and began to drift toward a parked car.

"Turn!" I yelled.

"Right or left?"

"Right. Right!"

We banked hard and started circling.

"Left!" I screamed, and we started circling in the opposite direction. "No, just a little!"

"A little right or a little left?"

"Right...No, left!" I laughed, and David laughed, too.

"David!" Mom screamed as she stepped out of the house.

Her shout surprised me and I turned to look. As I did, I accidentally pulled my left foot inward toward the wheel and caught it between the spokes. My foot was wrenched around until it jammed into the front fork, locking the wheel and stopping the bike dead. The back tire left the ground and we pitched forward. David somersaulted over me and slammed onto his back. The bike and I crashed in a tangled heap.

Later, in the hospital emergency room, a doctor explained that my twisted knee would keep me off my feet for a week.

"A week? It's not like the wheel ripped it off or anything!" David said.

"David!" Dad barked. Other than having the wind knocked out of him, David had escaped injury.

The doctor smiled and said to me, "Take it easy for a while and you'll be fine. And be careful in the future."

"Thanks," I said, and the doctor walked away.

Dad stroked my forehead, smiled, and said, "You were lucky it wasn't worse."

He glanced at Mom. Her dark expression must have said something to Dad, because he began to plead, "They're boys. They get bumped up. Accidents. You can't blame me for this."

"They didn't learn Blind Man Biking by accident!" she snapped.

"I didn't think they'd—"

" 'Didn't think' is right."

"That's not fair..."

"The boys copy everything you do. You have to be careful. When will you learn!"

Dad was mute for a moment, then his eyes got wide and he cried, "God, not Dee again. It's been years!"

Mom scowled at Dad.

"The war was on!" he protested.

"He was in a special program. Premed. He would have missed the fighting."

"You don't know that!"

"I know that he quit college and enlisted with you," Mom said, glaring at him.

Dad's hands fell to his sides.

"It was the war," he said, and he left the hospital room.

We never played Blind Man Biking again.

12

The rain tapered off to a drizzle. We surveyed our camp. Next to the shelter were six barbecue grills crudely fashioned from large metal drums sliced lengthwise and propped up on steel stilts. Beyond them was a gravel parking lot good for about twenty cars. A dirt road led from the lot and sliced through a meadow of weeds and disappeared into the trees beyond. On one side of the lot was a muddy playground with battered swings and a rusting slide. On the other side was a shack with VICTORY PARK painted across one wall.

We went to explore the shack. It was a bathroom. The fixtures were old, but the sink worked—cold water only—and the toilet flushed!

"We ain't leavin'!" David shouted, and we raced back to the canoe for our gear. We spread our things on a couple of tables and were relieved to discover that nearly everything was dry. Regularly wrapping our gear in our rain ponchos had proven to be a good precaution. Afterward, we hunted for wood to fuel one of the grills. The rain had soaked nearly everything, and it took an hour to find enough dry twigs and branches to make a fire. We discovered a field of tall corn and took six green-yellow ears. That evening, we dined on chili, corn, and Oreo cookies. The night was cool, and we ate snuggled into our sleeping bags, which we had spread on top of the picnic tables. The fire from the grill threw a soft light that flickered on us like the sun shimmering on the river.

"Man, this is a million times better than the army," David said. "In the field we gotta eat crappy canned stuff, stuff that shouldn't even be in a can, like eggs or turkey, and you can't even enjoy that, because you gotta race off for some kind of duty. Somebody's always screaming at you to hurry up. And you better, too! Once, a guy in the platoon—Bobby Culpepper—didn't finish his chow in time. Sergeant Gibson came over and spilled Culpepper's food on the ground and made him sit in it! 'Soldier,' he said, 'This chow's gotta get to your sorry asshole sometime and I'm just speeding it along.' Everybody cracked up."

"Is Culpepper a buddy?" I asked.

"No. Just a redneck I met at basic training. From somewhere in Maryland. Said he was in the Klan back home. Ku Klux Klan. I thought the Klan was way down in Alabama or Mississippi, but he said no, that it was up north, even in Maryland by the Delaware border. That's not very far from us! Anyway, he joined up with his cousin, another Maryland redneck. They were gonna be lifers and do thirty years in the service, but Culpepper found out he hated the army. Taking orders and all. And he couldn't stand living with colored guys. Man, what was he thinking when he joined up? I bet half the army is colored! Then his cousin got zapped by lightning with those two other guys."

"Were you friends with any of them?" I asked.

"Naw. The three of them and Culpepper hung out together. I'm surprised Culpepper didn't get blasted with them. God, what a mess. There are better ways of dying."

Were there really good and bad ways to die, I wondered.

We finished eating and slid deeper into our sleeping bags. The fire weakened and the pink-yellow glow from the grill dimmed.

"Is Culpepper going to Nam with you?" I asked.

"He's there now," David said. "I don't know why, but he got yanked from our platoon and went about a month ago. Man, I thought he was gonna cry when he got his orders. He ended up in a supply company stationed in Vung Tao. That's on the coast. It's supposed to be beautiful. I heard he's a bartender at an officers' club."

"That sounds better than getting shot at," I said.

"Yeah, until Charlie plants a bomb and blows the place up," David replied in a flat voice. "Charlie" was a nickname soldiers used for the enemy in South Vietnam.

"It's still gotta be safer than running around in the jungle," I insisted.

David just shrugged his shoulders.

"Maybe you'll be a bartender. Or an office worker," I suggested.

"I'm gonna end up a grunt in the boonies with an M16. Uncle Sam needs grunts," David replied.

"That isn't what you told Mom."

"I didn't want to scare her."

After a moment, I asked, "Are you? Scared, I mean."

"Nah. Well, maybe. A little. You'd be nuts otherwise," David answered. "But Sergeant Gibson says everything will be OK if you stay 'heads up and ass down.' "

I didn't think Sergeant Gibson was right, but I didn't say so. Instead I said, "Night, David."

"Night, Steve," David replied.

13

By mid-morning the next day, Victory Park was miles behind us. We had set out shortly after dawn and traveled without interruption. We didn't even stop to piss, instead risking the chancy stunt of doing it while standing in the floating canoe.

"If you get me wet, I'll kill you," David warned me when I carefully stood. "And I'm not talking about flipping the canoe."

More miles passed. The river grew wider, and the bridges that spanned it grew larger. Beneath a great concrete-and-steel-rigged one with suspended metal-grated roadways that made car tires sing, David and I hid our canoe and gear within the thick brush.

We had decided to reward our long morning of paddling with a restaurant lunch. After climbing the steep riverbank to the road, we set out for the town our map assured us was nearby. Cars and trucks flew past with a steady frequency that kept us off the road and on a grass shoulder.

David and I talked about the meal we were expecting to enjoy in the upcoming town; we were tired of canned food and peanut butter. We both loved to eat, and food was a safe subject, empty of conflict. With make-believe seriousness, we contested the merits of hot dogs with relish versus hot dogs with sauerkraut. I stood firmly in the relish camp. The argument was silly, but it helped pass the time.

The busy road cut a swath through a thick forest, its path following the gentle rises and dips of the land. After an hour of tramping, we still hadn't reached the town. David pulled a crumpled map from his back pocket.

"According to this, we should be there already," David said.

I didn't say anything. I was happy walking in the shadows of the tall trees that bordered the road. It was very quiet there, as if the forest muffled all sound.

We followed the winding road for another fifteen minutes until a large clearing opened before us, completely occupied by a sprawling camp of battered trucks and scuffed trailers. Men and women were everywhere, a battalion of workers as scruffy as their vehicles.

"Cool!" David said.

It was a carnival, or the makings of one, at least. There was a small half-built Ferris wheel, and the skeleton of a roller coaster lay near it like an unearthed fossil. The Whip, the Tornado, and other rides awaited assembly, and metal and plastic pieces were strewn in heaps. The midway was taking shape; wood and canvas were being framed together, and soon the dart toss, the milk can throw, and all the other petty larcenies masquerading as games would have homes.

The carnival was not a surprising discovery. Carnivals were a reassuring touchstone of the season. They made stops in towns everywhere.

We ambled into the middle of the activity. Each ride and game had its own gang of workers attending it. A dozen people scurried over the roller coaster with wrenches and hammers. Three others were constructing a makeshift pen and shoveling hay for the pony ride.

We watched the building of the Whip. Its crew cursed, laughed, then cursed again as they erected the ride. Their clothes were patched, their hair greasy, and their eyes red-rimmed like they hadn't slept in days. But they didn't show the least bit of weariness.

"Do these characters look kinda young to you?" David asked.

None appeared to be older than David. One, a fat blond-haired kid with an unlit cigarette hanging from the side of his mouth, looked my age.

"I don't know if I'd want to ride a ride that was made by a *kid*," I answered.

The carnival was rising on a field bordering the town we had been searching for. A simple painted sign at the edge of the field read MEMORIAL FIELD. But there were no ball fields, gazebos, or picnic tables, merely a grassy plain. The town consisted of a few rutted streets that intersected the road we had followed up from the river. A few tired-looking shops and run-down houses dotted the town. The windows of some of the houses were dressed with what appeared to be bedsheets. On the edge of town, adjacent to the carnival, was the Dew Drop Inn. Atop its roof was a sign with plastic letters of mixed sizes that proclaimed: HoME COOKIN', wEDNESDAY IS LADIES NIGHT, and, at the bottom, wE SUPPORT OUR BOYS IN vIETNAM.

"Maybe the Dew Drop serves hot dogs," David said, and he struck out for the restaurant. I followed, my stomach grumbling.

After a few steps, we heard someone call, "Hey, chief!"

We stopped and saw a man about thirty years old with long hair that spilled over his thick neck and broad shoulders. A leather necklace with bright colored feathers hung from his neck. His dungaree bell-bottoms were decorated with embroidered flowers. A half dozen teenagers trailed behind him. "Hey, chief!" he repeated, and he walked up to David.

"Listen, chief," he said, talking directly to David, "I'm shorthanded and we got to get this carnival up. I'm hiring some local guys to help out. How does five bucks sound— and all the free rides you want?" He guzzled the dregs of a Coke in one swallow, wiped his mouth with the back of his hand, and lifted his eyebrows to underscore his offer.

Before David could answer, the man pointed his finger at him and asked, "Army?"

David stiffened and hesitated before he finally said, "Yes," in a voice that was low and defensive.

"Yeah, thought so. The short hair always gives you away.

Air force, myself. Cargo chief for a C-130, two years in Germany. Got out in '64. Nam was just cranking up. Got buddies there now, though. Flying out of Bien Hoa, the big base near the capital, uh, Saigon. They got stories. Oh yes, they got stories. You been?"

"September," David replied.

"Not infantry, I hope?"

"Yeah."

"Geez, you don't want to be a grunt, bro! Bribe somebody if ya have to. Shoot your toe off. Anything. My buddies tell stories!"

"I'm not worried. My rifle company is tops. And my sergeant did two tours already."

The man just shook his head and said, "Well, I'm glad I did my bit already. Anyway, got this carnival to get up or I'd buy you a beer. So, you wanna work?"

David thought a few moments, then pointed to me with his thumb and asked, "What about him?"

The man looked at me as if noticing me for the first time. He frowned slightly as he ran his eyes up and down me. He rubbed one hand over his face like he was checking his beard, and exhaled slowly.

"Yeah. OK. Him, too," he finally said.

He surveyed the group around him. "You, you, you." He pointed to David and other strong-looking guys. "Come with me. The rest of you go see Rudy, he's that skinny little guy smoking a butt near the midway." With that, they headed away.

David started to leave, then he stopped and came over to me.

"This all right? If you want, we can forget it," he asked.

"I'll be OK. I'll catch up with you later," I answered.

He chased after his gang. The boss glanced at him, then called back to me, "Watch out, featherweight. I don't want you to get hurt."

As I went to meet Rudy, my face reddened.

14

I carried two cases of cola and two boxes of hot dogs to the back of the snack bar. The load was heavy, and I was forced to waddle over to the spot Rudy had pointed out. I had been helping Rudy ferry supplies all over the carnival for nearly four hours. Mostly it was prizes: trinkets, toys, stuffed animals. The prizes were old and dusty from being dragged from town to town; it was nearly impossible to win the ring-toss or knock over the milk cans, and players were rarely rewarded. We had to beat some of the stuffed animals like old rugs in order to clear the dust from them. I carried boxes of admission tickets, parts for the rides, and food for the snack bars: hot dogs, candy, soda, and popcorn.

The snack bars were really just shacks that held butane grills for heating hot dogs and hamburgers, and buckets filled with ice to serve with the drinks. I had stocked four snack bars and was about to head off to my fifth when David and the boss, whose name I had learned was Felix, walked past me. Felix seemed to be explaining something to David when they noticed me.

"Let's go, featherweight, I'm buying," Felix announced.

I looked at David, he nodded his head, and I fell into step with them.

Felix resumed his story: "I was just out of the air force and at loose ends and all. Figured I'd tool out to the West Coast, check it out. Bought a beat-up cycle, a Triumph Bonneville, for the trip. Then I heard that my uncle was laid up and there was nobody to run his carny. He had owned the carny for years, and I spent summers as a kid working for him. Had a blast! I figured that after two years of moving jeeps and cannons and people and important stuff all over Europe for the military, I could move a roller coaster and a portable toilet around New York and Pennsylvania. So I offered to run it, and he said sure. Been having a ball ever since. If it wasn't for this carny, I'd be working in an office somewhere, strangling in a tie and jacket, totally miserable."

Felix pulled a crumpled, greasy five dollar bill—my wages—from his pocket and handed it to me. I mouthed a silent "Thanks" and he nodded in response, but he didn't break the rhythm of his story.

"That was four years ago. My uncle never *did* come back to the carny. Decided it was time to retire, and sold the business to me. It was tough paying for it, but it became mine, free and clear, a year ago," he continued.

By the time Felix finished speaking, we were at the entrance to the Dew Drop Inn. He held the door open and we filed in. The carnival had drawn people from surrounding burgs, and the restaurant was crowded. We went over to the bar, and Felix wedged a place for us and caught the bartender's attention.

Felix looked uncertainly at me and then at David.

"Three beers?" Felix asked David.

"Two beers and a Coke," David replied.

The bartender heard the order and delivered our drinks.

Felix raised his glass in a toast and said, "Carny or not, this old vet couldn't let you leave without buying you a beer. Good luck in Nam."

Our three glasses met with a soft chime.

"Thanks," David replied.

Felix drained his glass in one long swallow.

"Sorry I can't hang with you longer, but the carny falls apart without me," he said. Then he put some cash on the counter and told the bartender, "Another round for my buddies, when they're ready."

He shook David's hand and said, "Take care of yourself. Really, bro, get outta the grunts." Then he nodded to me and left the bar.

"He's a good guy," David said. "I spent the whole time working with him. Helped finish the roller coaster. What did you do?"

He cut me off before I could begin.

"All the carny guys really respect Felix," he said. "You can tell by the way they joke around. Like he'd tell a bunch of guys to get their butts in gear and they'd start screaming and complaining, but in a joking way. Then Felix would threaten to fire them, but he'd be joking, too. Anyway, they'd all laugh and right away the guys would jump on whatever Felix wanted done. He's really cool. Reminds me a little of Sergeant Gibson."

When we finished our drinks, the bartender set down the second round Felix had bought us. I told David about the dusty stuffed animals and the boxes of snacks.

By the time I finished my second Coke, my stomach was feeling bubbly and uncomfortable. David, on the other hand, was relaxed and content. Before we could leave to have dinner—we hadn't eaten all day—the bartender placed a third beer in front of David.

"I heard you're going to Nam," the bartender explained. "This one's on me."

"Thanks!" David replied in a loud voice.

The bartender's remark and David's boisterousness attracted the attention of a gray-haired man and a woman who were standing beside us. They introduced themselves and explained how they had a nephew who was a sailor somewhere in Southeast Asia.

"Go navy!" David shouted.

They bought him another beer, as did a young man in a T-shirt and baggy bell-bottoms who stood to our other side and who had also overheard the bartender.

"More power to ya. No way I'd go," he announced as he handed David the glass of beer. "Head to Canada first."

"Well, if you do, Bobby, you'd better not come back to this town!" exclaimed the gray-haired man.

"It isn't World War II, Mr. Armstrong. Can't see the point of getting blown away for Vietnam," Bobby replied.

Mr. Armstrong snorted and turned away. Bobby shrugged his shoulders and wandered to the corner of the bar.

David sipped his beer and smiled. His eyes were glassy.

"Let's get some dogs at the carnival," he blurted as he finished his fifth beer. "Did you carry any cans of sauerkraut?"

"Dozens of them," I said, although I really didn't remember how many.

With his elbow tightly in my grasp, I directed him outside. The carnival had opened, and its garish lights were shining in the twilight. People were streaming toward it, and we joined the crowd. David followed a helter-skelter path of his own design, and I apologized to the people he crashed into. I was pretty sure David was drunk.

"Let's ride the Whip!" he yelled as we drew near it, but I steered him past.

We found a snack bar and I ordered two hot dogs, plain. I had a feeling sauerkraut wasn't the right thing for David to add to a stomach full of beer. I ordered a cup of coffee, too; people on TV were always giving drunks coffee to sober them up.

We ate the dogs but David spilled the coffee before swallowing much of it.

"Oops!" He laughed as the coffee splashed on the ground.

I left David to buy a replacement. When I returned, he was gone.

I plunged into the surrounding crowd. I circled the carnival and then pierced its heart. I stopped at the Whip and strained to find him among its riders, but he wasn't there. I walked the midway, hoping to spot him playing the ring-toss or the dart throw, but to no avail. The pressing crowds, the colored lights, the hurdy-gurdy noise, and David's disappearance made me feel like I was in a mad dream.

I found him beside a ticket booth, joking with a small knot of carny workers, including Felix and Rudy. David roared with laughter while the others looked on in bemusement.

"Hey Stevie, where'd ya go? Been lookin' all over for you!" he called. "Look, my buddy Felix is here!"

David wrapped one arm around Felix's neck and hugged him. Felix smiled good-naturedly.

"Stevie, I think you gotta get David to bed," Felix declared.

"No way! No bed!" David yelled, but everyone ignored him.

I nodded my head in agreement with Felix's suggestion, but not very convincingly, because Felix asked, "Problem?"

I quickly described the long hike back to the bridge, the scramble down the steep embankment, and the search for our hidden gear.

"You're not going to be able to do that at night," Felix said. "And not with him drunk, to boot."

He thought for a few moments and ran his hands through his hair. Then he turned to Rudy.

"Set them up in one of the empty trucks. No one will bother them there."

Rudy tugged David away.

"I don't want to go to sleep now!" he protested. But Rudy kept a firm grip on him until we reached one of the trucks I had unloaded earlier. Rudy made a mattress out of canvas tarpaulins and then laid David down.

"But I'm not sleepy!" he complained.

I thanked Rudy, and he returned to the carnival.

Despite David's protests, he fell asleep quickly. I climbed into the truck, settled down beside him, and stared out at the carnival. From a distance, it appeared somehow softer, its music more innocent. The sky above it shimmered in blue, green, and pink pastels as the carnival lights rose up like a fountain and splashed the low clouds with color. Muted laughter poured from the carnival in a lilting murmur, like water flowing over rocks. I fell asleep to the laughter.

I slept soundly until David awoke in the middle of the night, jumped from the truck, raced to the trees, and retched. He climbed back in and fell asleep without saying a word to me.

I was wide awake now. Staring into the night, I remembered Felix's remark about how his military buddies "had stories," and it repeated itself over and over again in my mind. Thinking what those stories might be and what they might mean for David frightened me. Vietnam didn't scare David, or so he said, but was he telling me the truth? Was he telling himself the truth?

The carnival had shut down for the night, and there were no lights, no sounds to distract me, and I stayed awake until dawn.

15

David sat up, moaned softly, and rubbed his eyes with the heels of his hands. He glanced at me, moaned again, and fell back to the tarpaulins.

"My head is pounding!" he groaned in a low, thick voice.

"Time to get back to the river. It's a beautiful day," I replied. "Let's find breakfast."

David groaned again.

"Never drink beer on an empty stomach," he said, looking at me with a grim expression that seemed to say that this was important information to be stored away for future use.

I hopped down from the back of the truck. David grunted and groaned but tumbled out after me. We stretched and let the morning sun warm us. I tramped toward the town and David followed, holding the sides of his head with both hands like it was a precious and fragile vase.

We cut through the carnival. A few carny workers were

picking up dirty cups, gooey paper plates, bent soda cans, candy wrappers, spilled popcorn, half-eaten hot dogs, and shattered candy apples.

We passed the Dew Drop Inn and headed to the center of the town. There we discovered an open general store. A police cruiser was parked in front. I recognized a few carny workers as they left the store with small brown bags, which I guessed held their breakfasts. The store was like the other general stores we had come upon, faded and sad with the air of impending abandonment. The floors needed sweeping and the shelves needed painting. A half dozen people stood in line to purchase coffee and a plastic-wrapped doughnut or a muffin from a cardboard box that sat beside the cash register.

We discovered Felix standing in one corner. He was talking to a state trooper, and both were sipping coffee. They seemed to be friends.

"God, I don't want to see Felix," David whispered. "I was an idiot yesterday."

David tried to be invisible as we searched for breakfast, but Felix spotted us and waved us over. David reluctantly joined him as I gathered doughnuts and chocolate milk. By the time I delivered the food to David, Felix was clapping a red-faced David on the back and dismissing his embarrassment.

"Hell, man, everybody gets blasted sometime!" Felix said. David smiled wanly.

"Morning, Stevie," Felix said, and I smiled. "Don't get too comfortable. Jack is gonna drive you guys back to your stuff."

Jack, the state trooper, nodded his head slightly in acknowledgment and said, "See you later, Felix. C'mon, boys, let's get going."

He shook Felix's hand and started for the door. We thanked Felix, said good-bye, and climbed into Jack's police cruiser, David up front and me in the back. We sped away and hurtled down the road. The cruiser was spotless, and I ate my breakfast gingerly, trying to avoid making a mess. David just held his doughnut.

"Appreciate the help," David said to Jack.

"Don't mind helping friends of Felix. Good guy. Known him for a few years. Dated my sister a while back. They split up, but he and I stayed friends. We hunt deer. Good shot. You hunt?"

David said he didn't, and the conversation died. The silence might have been uncomfortable had it gone on for too long, but Jack hit ninety—I saw the speedometer—and we were back to the canoe in moments. The cruiser skidded to a halt. We climbed out and thanked Jack.

"Stay out of trouble, boys," Jack said. It sounded as much like a warning as advice. He tipped his hat and raced off.

David stared at the departing police car. The early morning sun reflected off the cruiser and made it look like a comet as it receded from view.

"David?" I asked, trying to interrupt his daydreaming.

"Oh, sorry. My head's pounding and it hurts to think," he replied.

"Let's get to our stuff, OK?" I said, and I clambered down

the embankment, toward the canoe. I turned around to make sure David was following. He was unsteady, clumsily balancing doughnut in one hand and chocolate milk in the other. He tripped a few times. When the slope dropped steeply near the riverbank, his balance deserted him entirely. His arms windmilled furiously, and chocolate milk sprayed everywhere. Then he pitched headlong and landed with a splat on his chest and face in the muck and nettles.

I was afraid to say a word.

"Damn, damn, damn," he whispered.

"You OK?" I finally asked.

He stood up and looked down at himself. His front was slick and filthy but his back was clean; he resembled a giant chocolate-frosted gingerbread man.

"Look at me," he said with a note of defeat in his voice.

His doughnut was squashed against his shoulder. I walked up to him and peeled the doughnut off him slowly, like I was removing an unexploded bomb. I held the smashed cake between my thumb and forefinger. Only custard held it together. A few pebbles were embedded in it, and bits of acorn, too.

"You gonna eat this?" I asked.

He started laughing, and I joined in. It was good to hear it.

"Score another one for Stevie," he chuckled.

He stripped off his pants and shirt and tossed them into the river. He followed his clothes into the water. While he got clean, I uncovered our gear, intending to dig out a towel and clean clothes for him.

"Oh, crap!" I barked. "Something ate our food!"

David came out of the water and poked through the remains of our food pack. Bits of crackers, cookies, and cereal coated the bottom of the bag. The bags and boxes were torn or bitten open and empty. Only the cans and jars were untouched.

"Raccoons," he said. "Look."

There were paw prints in the soft earth all around the canoe.

"Should have known better," he rebuked himself. "The little bandits get into everything. We'll have to shop again at the next town. Get some aspirin, too. Man, I didn't know a few beers on an empty stomach could hammer me so bad."

David got dressed, and I tidied our gear and dragged the canoe into the water. Then David got in.

"You take the stern," he said. "I'm beat."

I was surprised. David had always treated the rear seat as if it were his birthright.

"C'mon, Steve. Let's get going," he said.

I gripped the canoe and, in one graceful movement, launched it free of the riverbank as I hopped into the stern. I snatched up the paddle and drove the canoe forward with a deep, strong stroke. I turned the paddle in the water and steered the canoe into a sweeping curve that placed us at the center of the river. I stroked heavily and outran the current, thrilled by my own power.

David nestled himself amidst the gear and napped.

16

"More rain?" David said, glancing at the leaden sky as he handed me two bags of groceries. I stowed them as David climbed into the canoe with me. We had found a general store, and I had waited with the canoe while David shopped.

As we slipped back into the river's current, David said, "There was a phone at the store. I called Mom. Just to let her know we're OK. She was kinda PO'd that we hadn't called sooner. I told her we'd try to call tomorrow so you could speak with her."

Rain started to fall. It began light and feathery. After a few minutes it strengthened, hammering us with heavy drops.

"This sucks!" David screamed.

"Sucks!" I answered.

"Sucks!" we bellowed together.

Laughing, we guided the canoe to a patch of weeds nestled beside the river.

We erected a small lean-to between two small trees and crammed our gear and ourselves beneath it. A chilly wind stirred the air, and we crawled into our sleeping bags to escape the cold. The sober weather dampened our conversation; we didn't speak for more than an hour.

David squirmed inside his sleeping bag as he searched for a comfortable position. He pulled a map from his pack, studied it for a moment, and then thrust it away.

"This is as bad as the army," he moaned.

I had no idea what he was talking about and merely shrugged my shoulders.

"From the very first day, you spend most of your time *waiting* in the army," he explained. "Just waiting. Waiting for orders. Waiting for chow. Waiting for officers. Waiting and more waiting. It's really boring.

"Once we stood at attention for three and a half hours on the parade ground waiting for a general to arrive. He never did, by the way. Guys were fainting left and right. Guys were puking. The guy in front of me was standing in a puddle. He had pissed in his pants! It was awful.

"Another time, we made a twelve-mile night march. Carrying a full pack and a rifle. An hour into the hike, that stuff felt like a million tons. Some guys tried to drop out, but we were ordered to drag them along. I carried a buddy's rifle for half the march 'cause he was dragging tail. We arrived at a field where there were supposed to be trucks to carry us back to camp. No trucks! Nothing! We waited from dawn till noon, then the idiot captain in charge of the company decided we should march back. That really blew!"

"Sounds like the time Dad was supposed to meet us at the train station," I said.

"Huh? Oh yeah, I almost forgot about that!" David replied.

Several years ago, Mom was away and Dad made a plan to meet David and me at the train station on his way home from work, after which he would take us for a Chinese dinner. David and I got to the station early and greeted the passengers departing the 5:40, expecting Dad to be among them. But he never appeared. The 6:10 and the 6:38 disgorged their commuters, but he never appeared. I started to cry and wanted to go home, but David thought it was best that we stay. As each new train arrived, we frantically searched for Dad. When he finally stepped from the 9:40 train, we were squatting against the station wall, half asleep.

"He felt like a total jerk for forgetting about us," David remembered, laughing.

"Yeah, and then he took us for lobster and made us promise not to tell Mom!" I chuckled. "Then *he* admitted it to her a few weeks later, and she got really pissed and called him a peckerhead!"

David and I rolled with laughter and nearly collapsed our fragile lean-to.

"I'd never heard Mom talk like that. She was really ticked off!" I said. "You'd think Dad would have had the sense to keep his mouth shut."

"Sometimes you got to take your lumps for your mistakes. That's what being a man is all about," David replied. "At least that's what Sergeant Gibson says.

"That time when the trucks never came for my company,"

David said, the excitement in his voice rising, "and we had to march back, we were beat! Everyone knew it was the captain's fault. I mean *everyone* knows he's a total screwup! Anyway, when we got back to camp, he tried to make out like it was Sergeant Gibson's mistake, said the sergeant was the ranking NCO and should have made sure the trucks were ordered.

"You gotta understand the sergeant has seen a lot of bad stuff and isn't afraid of anything. In Nam, his unit was over-run by the VC and he had to hide beneath the bodies of dead buddies. So he marched up to the captain and told him that it was the captain's responsibility and why doesn't he *start acting like a man*!

"Nobody in the company had ever heard an NCO talk to an officer like that, so we were ready to burst wondering what was going to happen. Next thing you know, the captain turns red and then starts screaming, 'How dare you address me that way! I'll have your stripes! I'll bust you down to private!' and on and on, making an awful racket.

"Sergeant Gibson just stood there, at parade rest, not even looking at the captain. That really set the captain off, and he began to holler and rant even more. I thought he was going to have a heart attack. Finally a colonel drove past in a jeep, slammed on his brakes, and leaped out to see what the ruckus was about. Everybody snapped to attention, except the captain, who was so hysterical that he didn't even notice the colonel was there.

"Finally the colonel shouted, 'Control yourself, captain!'

and the captain jumped to attention and saluted. Then the colonel approached the captain real slowly and pushed his face right up against the captain's, said something, I don't know what, 'cause he just whispered it. The captain does an about-face and marches quick-time off the parade ground like he's heard the voice of God. Man, I wish I knew what the colonel said!

"The colonel turns to Sergeant Gibson and tells him to dismiss the men, then jumps back in his jeep and drives away."

"So Gibson won out over the captain," I interrupted.

"Yeah, but *this* is the cool part of the story," David continued. "When the colonel left, the company started cheering. Sergeant Gibson cut us off and said, 'The next sonofabitch who cheers will be doing push-ups and jumping jacks till he's mustered out of the army!'"

David looked at me expectantly, earnestly.

"I don't get it," I admitted after a moment.

"Don't you see?" David replied. "He didn't do it for us. He wasn't showing off. He did it for himself. He was going to stand up for what was right *no matter what.*"

17

David's elbow jabbed my ribs, awaking me with a start. I was sore and my head ached from a lack of sleep. We had spent the night pressed together beneath the small lean-to, and David's knees and arms had pummeled me as he slept fitfully.

It was morning. A fine gray mist had replaced the rain, and an earthy perfume filled the air.

I gave David a shove and he awoke with a grumble. We ate breakfast and disassembled our camp. When we lifted our ground cover, a poncho placed under our sleeping bags, we discovered a couple dozen slugs attached to its underside. The glistening gray thumb-sized things were stuck to the poncho, and I felt like I might puke when we whacked them with sticks to remove them.

We set out. The scenery along the river became grittier. Car and truck dealerships appeared, as did oil storage tanks and decrepit silos. Warehouses sprang up. We passed a huge junkyard, a giant automobile graveyard. It was irresistible and we beached the canoe to explore. Disemboweled automobiles were everywhere. The ground was black with spilled oil that leached into the river in great rainbow-colored arcs of greasy sluice. We explored the yard and met a gray-and-brown mongrel dog chained to a fence. He looked at us with bored eyes, then flopped on his side and went to sleep.

Most of the cars—wrecks, really—were squashed flat and stacked five high. Transmissions, axles, and driveshafts poked from them like fractured limbs. Wheels, cogs, bolts, pans, belts, springs, all kinds of rubbish littered the ground and made crunching sounds as we walked on them. Most of the vehicles were from the fifties and sixties, but there were some really old cars, too, ancient Fords and Chevys. We discovered a moss-green Packard (David thought it was a '39) and climbed into it. The steering wheel was immense, big enough to steer a steamship. The backseat was like a living room sofa, with thick, spongy cushions. A dusty brown cloud rose from it and filled the car when we sat in it.

Nearby were the cab and fenders of a Model T Ford. The engine and seats were gone and the windows were smashed out. Sitting there, gutted and empty, the dead Ford seemed haunted.

A khaki-colored Studebaker caught our eye. It was shaped like a rocket ship and appeared to be undamaged and fine enough to drive away, had it not been balanced atop a pile of five flattened wrecks. The stack sat apart from other piles and made kind of an automobile totem. We approached it, David on one side and me on the other.

"That's the coolest car ever," David said in a hushed, reverential tone. He looked at it for a long while, then scrambled up the stack.

"Race you!" he taunted. "King of the hill!"

I leaped onto the pile and climbed. The metal and plastic didn't offer many hand- or footholds, and it was a struggle. David dove into the Studebaker through the driver's window and I followed through the passenger door. David slipped behind the steering wheel and pounded the dead horn.

"Honk. Hooonnnkkk!" he shouted. "I'm king of the hill. I'm king of the Studebaker!"

"Cheater! You had a head start!" I laughed.

"Sore loser!"

We joked and hollered and laughed. David squirmed to the backseat and I slid into the driver's seat, taking my turn to "honk" the horn with high sharp brays. We bounced inside the car like monkeys in a box, giggling and shouting the whole while. Breathless, we slumped in the backseat and threw our legs over the front seat.

"What a view," David said as he scanned the surroundings.

What a view it was—ugly and dark. The junkyard had scarred the landscape.

"Let's get the hell out of here," David announced, and he threw open the passenger door. He scuttled out and I followed. The pile of cars tilted and quivered. Simultaneously we realized our mistake: we had climbed the pile on opposite sides and hadn't disturbed its balance, but now our combined weight on one side promised to topple it.

David clambered down as fast as he could; it looked like he was sliding along the jagged wrecks. I started down, felt the pile falling, and leaped off. I hit the ground with a thud, almost knocking myself senseless. David grabbed my shirt and dragged me away from the pile, which tilted wildly. Then the Studebaker crashed down, first onto its side, then it flopped on its roof, unleashing an enormous cloud of dirt.

My ribs hurt and I lifted my shirt; a long scar ran diagonally from my left nipple to my right hip. I didn't remember being cut, and it only mildly stung. Blood oozed from it, and a few droplets slid down my torso like raindrops on a wet window.

I stared at the car, then made an invisible mark in the air with my finger.

"Score one for David," I said.

"For what?" he said flatly, and he straightened himself.

"For pulling me away from—"

"The car never came close," he snapped. "I was just helping you up."

"Well, thanks anyway," I mumbled.

He shrugged and came over to examine my wound.

"Let's see," he said. He bunched up a corner of his shirt and used it to gently wipe the thin, uneven lines of blood that had dribbled down my body. "Looks nasty. Does it hurt?"

"Naw. Not really."

David looked at it for a few moments and poked at it tenderly a couple of times.

"You ever have a tetanus shot?" he asked.

"I don't remember. You think I need one?" I replied.

"There's a ton of dirt and rust around. I think it would be good to know if you've had one."

I held my shirt up and looked at the dripping cut. Tetanus scared me, although I had never met anyone who had had it, and knew nothing about it other than that it was called lockjaw, whatever that meant.

"I don't remember! What am I gonna do?" I sputtered.

"Calm down! We'll figure something out," he barked.

"Should we call Mom and Dad? They'd know if I had a tetanus shot," I bleated.

"Hell no!" David shot back. "You know how nuts Mom is, how she worries. Do you want to give her a heart attack?"

We walked back to the canoe.

"What about you? You're cut, too," I said. His hands and one knee bled lightly; I guessed it was from his slide down the pile.

"I got a million shots when I went into the army. Tetanus was one of them," he said. "Sergeant Gibson says the army pumps you up with so much juice that they're really just trying to embalm you early to save time once you're killed."

David laughed, but the joke escaped me so I didn't.

We set out on the river again. The junkyard disappeared from sight. My wound hurt when I paddled, and I wanted to ask David if he had figured out the tetanus thing, but I kept quiet.

"We'll find a doctor," David announced. "There's a large town just downriver. Should be a doctor there."

"We can do that?" I asked.

"Why not?" he replied.

He stroked his paddle deeply and the canoe charged forward. I added my paddle to the river, and as I did, a pain cut across my body.

18

We reached the town in mid-afternoon. It could have been made quaint with a little effort, but instead it was shopworn and tired. Slate-roofed houses along its wide streets wore faded paint, and the stately buildings occupying its downtown were grimy. The marble columns of the town hall were stained and chipped. Dusty bare spots scarred the large lawn of the town square, and the wrought-iron fence that surrounded it was rusting.

We stashed the canoe just beyond the town, in heavy brush beside a lumberyard. Nearby was a road that ran beside the river. As we followed it back toward the town, we passed a weed-choked cemetery, its shaggy grass an unkempt carpet for leaning headstones.

"You can tell how much pride a town has by the way it cares for its graveyard," David said.

"Sergeant Gibson?" I asked.

"Huh?"

"Sergeant Gibson, he said that?"

"Oh . . . yeah," David replied, and his face reddened. "He's always talking about how the army takes care of its own, right down to burying you in a beautiful place like Arlington Cemetery," David explained. "To show respect for those who served."

Dad had taken us to Washington once and we visited Arlington Cemetery. It was stunning, but I remembered thinking at the time how sad it seemed.

We passed a library, a big red brick building with "1893" carved into its cornerstone. It had giant windows of translucent glass; lights from within the library made them glow pale yellow.

"They'll have a phone book there," David explained, and he led me inside. "We can check for doctors."

The librarian, a heavyset woman with dark, tired eyes, listlessly pointed in the direction of the phone book after we described our dilemma. Three doctors were listed. We asked the librarian which was closest. She sighed deeply, as if burdened by great effort, and told us Dr. Murtogg's office was around the block.

Murtogg's office occupied a corner of a very large Victorian house. A sign directed us to a side entrance and we discovered leather padded chairs lining a dark, wood-paneled waiting room. It was empty. On the far side of the room was another door. Beside it was a receptionist's window, from which a gaunt gray woman whose hair was tied tightly in a bun watched us. Her eyebrows lifted and her forehead furrowed all the way to her tightly pulled-back hair as we approached.

"Can we see the doctor, please?" David said.

The woman pursed her colorless lips. Her nose, sharp enough to spear an olive, rose slightly and she looked down its length at us.

"My brother's cut," David explained. I lifted my shirt.

"Are you a patient of the doctor?" she asked, ignoring my cut. Her tone made it perfectly clear that she already knew the answer.

"No," David answered. "But—"

"Then you must return with your parents. A responsible party must accompany children before the doctor can see them," the woman said. She lowered her head and returned to her paperwork.

I started to leave but David just stood there, his eyes moving as if searching his mind for an idea. Then he dug his hand into his back pocket, removed his wallet, and lifted a card from it. He flung the card down on the woman's desk. Her head snapped up.

"What do—?" she spat.

"That's my army identity card. I am nineteen years old and a member of the armed forces of the United States," he announced loudly. "I am my brother's legal guardian and want medical attention for him. Do I get it or do I notify the authorities?"

She examined the card, flipping it over several times,

struggling to measure its authenticity. She looked up and her eyes drilled David, who met her stare. Red-faced and sputtering under her breath, she left her seat and disappeared down a hallway, still holding David's ID.

I was mute. What havoc had David unleashed? I looked at him and he was grinning.

"Did you see the way she jumped?" He giggled. "'Legal guardian!' 'Notify the authorities!' Man, what a jerk!"

I had been fooled by David's nerve, too, but I started to laugh. The woman returned, opened the door, and told us to go to the examination room at the end of the hall. We were almost bursting as we passed her; she tried to revive her earlier air of indifference but couldn't stop herself from scowling.

David and I were still smiling when the doctor entered the examination room. He looked to be about Dad's age and appeared to be very fit; the muscles in his neck reminded me of our high school wrestling coach. Behind his wire-framed glasses were narrow eyes absent of laugh lines.

"Let's see," he said to me through thin, unsmiling lips. I lifted my shirt. "How'd this happen?"

"He fell," David said before I could answer.

Before he continued his examination, Murtogg handed David back his ID.

"Army, huh?" he asked David while fingering my wound.

"Yes, sir," David replied.

"You're a rare breed, son," Murtogg said. "No one wants to serve any more. Everybody's running off to college, hiding in

Canada, or otherwise angling to beat the draft. You wouldn't believe the number of brats who want me to give them medical deferments to get them out of the army. The gimmicks they use! One kid set off firecrackers in the trunk of his car while his head was stuck in to induce deafness. Another ate a box—a whole box, mind you!—of laxatives. They try to flatten their feet by jumping from roofs, or carry weights to induce a hernia. I send them all packing!"

While he spoke, he swabbed my wound with antiseptic roughly and I flinched.

"It's a shame fine boys like you have to serve while cowards ride free," he declared as he prepared a needle.

"This tetanus shot will square you up," he said, and he plunged it into my arm. A dull, hot pain accompanied the serum as it was pumped in, and I winced.

"Maybe they're smarter," David remarked.

"What are you talking about?" Murtogg asked.

"The ones trying to beat the army," David replied quietly. "Maybe trying to keep your ass from getting blown away is smarter."

David's words surprised me. Had he had second thoughts about enlisting?

Murtogg looked at David goggle-eyed.

"Nonsense!" he barked. "Your country calls and you go. There's nothing to figure. I was drafted. I served. Fort Leonard Wood. The army hospital. Two years working for the government instead of building my practice. Now it's your turn. And when your brother comes of age, you'll explain the rules to him, you'll make sure he does his bit. That's how it works."

"Getting blown away for eternity isn't two years in Arkansas," David replied.

Dr. Murtogg's face reddened. He snorted, turned his back to David, and jotted something on a medical form.

"Give this to the woman at the desk," Murtogg snapped, handing me the form, and he tried to exit the room but David blocked him.

"And if my brother decides he wants to dress up like a woman to beat the army, I'll buy him high heels and stockings," he said.

Murtogg stepped around him and stomped out of the room.

We were back on the street in minutes.

"David," I said.

"Yeah?"

"Can you get me flats instead of heels? They hurt when I walk."

"You start dressing like a girl and I'll knock your block off!"

19

We bought a bag of groceries and returned to the beached canoe. The sun was still warm, and its heat felt good. I rooted through the groceries and lifted out drinks. The sharp scream of a saw ripping wood carried from the neighboring lumberyard. Castaway lumber littered the nearby ground.

David looked at the discarded wood for a while, then said, "Let's drift tonight."

I stared at him blankly.

"We'll let the canoe drift through the night," he explained. "We'll use some of this lumber to make an outrigger to keep the canoe from tipping, and then we can sleep on our packs while we're drifting. We're going to have to spend the night here otherwise, and this is a crappy campsite! As a matter of fact, this whole town bites, and so do all the morons in it. If we use an outrigger, we can canoe through the night and get away from this place."

The idea grabbed me, and the two of us set to work. We rummaged through the lumber and found a thick eight-foot beam. A crack running along its length had ruined it for construction, but it was perfect for our outrigger. Using some heavy hemp cord we also found, we tied two smaller pieces of wood close to the ends of the beam so that the three pieces formed a shape like a large block-letter C. We lashed the short pieces to the canoe, and the beam floated beside it. Once in the water, our remodeled craft tilted slightly toward the outrigger side but was otherwise remarkably stable. Satisfied our work, we set out.

We made an early dinner of thick ham sandwiches. Our paddles were stowed, and the canoe found its own lazy course. We used our packs as cushions and comfortably awaited dusk. The busy day and the effortless travel made us sleepy, and we napped.

When I awoke, night had fallen. The world around me had disappeared, replaced by a blanketing darkness that was complete and blinding. No moonlight intruded on the blackness, and not even tiny pinpricks of stars could be seen. I waited for my eyes to adjust to the blackness and struggled to recognize the familiar outline of the passing shore or a looming tree. I waited and I struggled and I saw...nothing.

It was completely black. In the suburban world I knew, streetlights and home lights radiated a surplus brightness that softened the hardest darkness. Now, on the river, under a moonless sky that swallowed even the boldest stars, there was nothing to see, and that nothingness frightened me.

I heard David snoring softly. His presence was comforting. Almost.

"David," I said, hoping to wake him, hoping his voice would soothe my jangled nerves. "David."

"Huh, whaaa…Wow!" he exclaimed when confronted with the pitch blackness. "Steve, you there?"

"I can't see a thing."

"It's creepy, isn't it? Like you're blind. I never knew it could get this dark until the army, when I went on night maneuvers. One time, it was so pitch black that most of the platoon got lost and I couldn't find my way out of a pond for a half-hour. What a mess! Get the flashlights."

We pawed inside our packs. I heard the gentle *plop* of something falling into the river.

"What was that?" I asked.

"I haven't the slightest idea," he answered.

After several minutes David found his flashlight, and with its light I easily uncovered my own. Their beams revealed disk-shaped glimpses of our surroundings.

"Let's not waste the batteries," David said, and his light disappeared with a click. I reluctantly followed his instructions and we were once more draped in perfect blackness.

Something—a fish?—splashed out of and back into the water. A dog sang out with a chilling howl that sounded far off and close by at the same time. An immense choir of insects droned in relentless harmony.

We sailed in and out of pockets of cold air. Everything became clammy; when I touched the canoe, I felt a thin skin of moisture.

"Look," David said, forgetting for a moment that I had no notion of the direction he wished me to look in. "To the right. To the right of the front of the canoe."

I saw an enormous ghost towering hundreds of feet in the evening sky. Not a real ghost, but the telltale incandescence of a far-off town that rose like steam from a pot. It percolated through low clouds, its brightness strengthening and diminishing haphazardly.

As I watched it, I heard running water, and then something clubbed my forehead. The force and surprise of it made me grunt and I nearly somersaulted out of the canoe.

"You OK?" David called, and he switched on his flashlight and caught me in its beam. I mumbled that I was fine and turned on my flashlight as well.

The canoe had drifted to the outside of a sweeping bend in the river. As we neared the riverbank, an overhanging tree branch had struck me. We had collided with a floating tangle of branches and wood and refuse, the flotsam and jetsam of the river. The river bubbled through it, making a sound like a running faucet.

"Crap!" David exclaimed. "Hold this," he instructed, handing me his flashlight. I held the two lights and David tore at the trap.

The refuse around us was slimy and smelled of rot. David pulled branches and wood away, but the current pulled us firmly against different pieces that took hold of us anew. The outrigger slipped beneath the pile-up as we were crushed into the tangle. The canoe tilted dangerously and we shipped water.

"Damn! Damn! Damn!" David roared.

He snatched an oar by the blade, plunged it into the water, and felt for the bottom. It was about four and a half feet deep. Satisfied, David hopped into the water and struggled to wrestle us free.

"Make sure those lights stay on!" he barked. The thought of standing in the river in total darkness would have given me the willies, too.

The canoe tilted even more sharply. David leaned into the canoe, plunged his hand into one of the packs, and removed the buck knife. He sawed at the outrigger ropes, but the blade slid over the wet, greasy cords. David bore down and tried again. This time, he sliced them. Separated from the outrigger, the canoe again became buoyant. David walked us clear of the obstruction.

"I'm coming in, steady us," he ordered. I used my body as a counterweight to prevent us from capsizing as he pulled himself back into the canoe. He settled himself and we set off downstream. David paddled and I held the flashlights like headlights. To the east, a thin band of royal blue outlined the horizon. It was the start of a new day.

20

Dawn arrived with a weak light. Mist blanketed the river, and everything around us was murky. We paddled hesitantly, as if exploring the edges of a dream. Slowly the riverbank revealed itself, the trees and bushes found edges, and the slopes of green-gray hills rose around us. Ahead, a narrow bridge appeared. Houses were clustered at one end.

We drifted beneath the bridge, and sweat from its rusty metal frame dripped on us. The river turned sharply and curled behind the town. We landed the canoe on a short sandy beach and stowed it in some high weeds. A dirt path led us through ragged grass to a collection of shabby houses on both sides of a rutted country road. Near the bridge was a gas station and a large whitewashed building. Cars and pickup trucks were parked beside the building, and we could hear people inside talking.

"It's Sunday. Maybe it's a church," I said.

"Don't be a dope. It's six o'clock in the morning, and that's a general store, not a church," David answered.

We approached the building. A faded sign that read SNAKE LANDING GENERAL STORE hung above its large front window. A series of hand-drawn letters spelling out COLD BEER were taped to the glass panes. Next to the window was a door; an OPEN sign hung from its knob, but the door was locked.

We pressed our foreheads against the window and looked in. The store was unlit. Beyond its dark shelves were the dim lights of a saloon, where about a dozen men were gathered at a worn bar. Beer bottles littered the counter, and cigarette smoke drifted in clouds.

"C'mon," David said. He headed to another door along the side of the building, one closer to the bar. SNAKE LANDING BAR AND GRILL was hand-painted on it. It was open, and David and I entered.

The musky odor of beer, sweat, and smoke enveloped us. Battered tables and chairs sat haphazardly about the floor, and an old jukebox stood opposite the bar. The patrons were talking in loud voices. I had the impression they had been there all night. They ignored our arrival, except for the bartender, who deliberately sauntered toward us from the far end of the bar.

"Help you boys?" he asked in a flat, indifferent tone.

"Can we get breakfast? Something to eat?" David replied. "We've been on the river all night."

"All night on the river? What the hell are you boys up to?" asked a voice from behind us.

We turned and met the questioning, unfocused eyes of a

middle-aged man whose gray hair had retreated far up his forehead. He held a can of beer in one hand and the tiny stub of a cigarette in the other.

"My brother and I came down from Cooperstown. We're heading downriver toward Wilkes-Barre."

"Damn! You don't say! Hey, Roy. C'mere. These boys rafted down from Cooperstown!"

Roy, a larger, balder middle-aged man, plodded over to us.

"Rafted? Whatthehellyoutalkin'?" grunted Roy. His face was shiny with sweat.

David corrected the first man about our canoe trip and our plans. Three other men drifted over to listen.

I felt a hand on my shoulder. It was the bartender's.

"I ain't grilling anything at this hour. Grab what interests you from the store," he said.

I explored the darkened shelves of the store and returned with a quart of orange juice and a stack of cellophane-wrapped pastries. David and eight men were crowded around a table near the bar. I sat next to David in a chair he had saved for me.

"Them yellow sonsabitches would sneak into our foxholes at night and try to slit our throats, but we killed their sorry asses, cut off their ears and hanged 'em from a string!" snarled a big muscular man with short gray hair and gun-metal-blue eyes. His meaty hand lifted a full glass of beer to his mouth, and he swallowed its contents in one large gulp.

"At Iwo, the Seabees drove bulldozers over the Nips and flattened 'em like pancakes." Roy laughed.

I guessed that the men had learned of David and Vietnam and seized the opportunity to tell war stories.

Jim, a thin man with bony, tobacco-stained hands, had been an army artillery man in France in '44. Roy was with a navy construction battalion and had landed at Iwo Jima. The beefy man with blue eyes, whom everyone called Crock, was a marine who had fought at Okinawa. David and I listened until the tales—some real, some imagined—petered out.

Crock ended the reminiscing with a simple "Man, that was something." It was clear that he was speaking for them all, that those days of World War II had been something— something special and vital. Was it odd that war could be remembered so fondly?

"I stayed in the marines after the war," Crock added. "Was gonna be a lifer but I got out when they got rid of separate white and colored units. Military got to be *desegregated*, they said, and let all the coloreds just mix right in. What crap! That faggot Roosevelt's idea." The other men grunted in agreement.

"Truman," I said, dredging up a fact learned in the previous year's history class.

Crock's head turned toward me like the turret of a battleship. His eyes narrowed and his jaw tensed. The other men shifted in their seats, and everyone stared at me.

"President Truman," I explained. "He was the one who desegregated the military, not President Roos—"

"Truman! Roosevelt! I don't give a crap who did it!" Crock growled. His cold eyes pinned me to my seat. "Niggers ruined the marines, and now they're trying to ruin the country. Just last week in Scranton, a buncha nig—"

"My top sergeant is a black guy," David interrupted.

Crock's glare shifted from me to David.

"He served two tours in Nam."

Crock looked at David quizzically.

"Deep in the boonies. Two silver stars. Saved his platoon's butt."

Crock stared at David, who returned his gaze evenly. After a long pause, Crock laughed, but there was no mirth in it.

"A regular hero, huh? Well, we won our war, boy, without nigger heroes!" Crock spat. "How're you and the coloreds doin' with yours?" His eyes narrowed. "You and your kind can't hold a candle to us. We whipped the Japs! And the Krauts! We beat the Depression! We—"

"Got us into Vietnam," said David, impaling Crock's tirade with a reminder of America's unloved, unhappy war. The war everyone wished would *just go away*. But it hadn't gone away. It ground on, like a bad business skirting bankruptcy, indenturing the nation's youngsters to its grim enterprise.

David pushed away from the table, walked to the bar, and paid for our breakfast. Crock's face reddened and his eyes drilled David.

I rose from my chair and moved to join David. I tried to pass Crock, but he tilted his chair backward and blocked my path.

He grinned and hissed, "Them gooks are gonna send your brother home in a bag."

Something putrid leaked into my throat.

"Screw you!" I shouted and shoved Crock, who was still balanced on the back legs of his chair.

The push sent him crashing to the floor. Grunting and furious, he scrambled to his feet and cocked his fists. David smashed into him from behind and sent him flying into the table. People, beer bottles, glasses, ashtrays went tumbling. A few men lay sprawled in puddles of warm beer that were cloudy with dirt and ashes. Crock howled. His nose was spurting blood.

The bartender grabbed a baseball bat from behind the counter and charged.

"Come on, Stevie!" David yelled, and he yanked me out the door by my T-shirt.

21

We sprinted down the street, darted between two houses, plunged down a bushy embankment, and raced along the greasy riverbank. David fell but was back on his feet before I could stop and help him. When we reached the canoe, my chest was pounding but I felt giddy, too.

"What did you think you were *doing* back there?" David demanded.

His anger hurt me. *Defending you!* I thought to myself, and was about to say so when, behind us, men shouted and car motors roared.

David cocked his head slightly, the way rabbits do when they are trying to identify a mysterious sound.

"Move!" he yelled.

We dragged the canoe from the brush, hurled it into the river, and threw ourselves aboard. We paddled madly. Three men raced to the shore; each carried a slat or a pipe. One, ex–artillery man Jim, gasped for air and gave us the finger.

"Paddle!" David barked.

Three battered sedans raced past us. Crock was driving one of them. The road and the river ran beside each other, like tines in a fork, for about a hundred yards, and then parted in opposing right-angle turns. At the bend, rocks and boulders scarred the river like acne. The water wasn't deep enough to float the canoe, and it was shallow enough for angry men with clubs to wade. My chest and throat tightened.

"It's low ahead!" I croaked.

"Paddle!" he answered.

The cars skidded to a halt at the curve. Eight men leaped out and plunged into the heavy brush that separated the road from the river.

We paddled to the far side of the river until we ground to a halt, then jumped into the shallow water. I yanked the front of the canoe upward and forward over the gravelly bottom while David pushed from behind using his shoulder. The canoe made a sound like knives being sharpened.

Crock and the others emerged from the bushes and vaulted into the water, waving metal pipes, broomsticks, and two-by-fours. The men stumbled in the thigh-deep water; water sprayed everywhere in sloppy showers.

We dragged the canoe over puddles, small rocks, and damp sand. My arms and lungs burned. David grunted.

The men found their feet and plowed through the water. Crock dropped the pipe he was carrying and tore at the water with cupped hands in an effort to propel himself. He raced ahead of the others, knees pumping, feet high-stepping clear of the water. The distance between us shrank. He stumbled on loose rocks and nearly fell, but he kept coming.

I panted wildly. My hands were numb and weak, and I barely kept my grip on the canoe. Suddenly the river bottom fell away and I pitched backward into waist-high water. I scrambled into the front of the canoe as David launched us forward.

"Go! Go! Go!" David hollered, and he flopped in behind me. He snatched up his paddle and chopped at the water. With each stroke, a low growl hissed through his clenched teeth.

I glanced back. Crock was charging hard. I fought the crazy thought that he was growing, ballooning to a monstrous size, like a genie emerging from a bottle. His feet pounded the water and made explosions of spray and foam. His face was twisted into a teeth-baring snarl. Just yards behind us, he leaped forward and hurtled through the air, his body extended, his arms outstretched, and his fingers splayed like talons, reaching for the back of the canoe. I froze. There was a huge splash, and the stern of the canoe plunged downward as the bow leaped up. I waited to be thrown into the river, but instead felt the canoe surf forward. I wiped the water from my eyes. David was in the back of the canoe, wide-eyed. And in the river behind him, thrashing the water as poor swimmers do, was Crock.

He had fallen short!

David and I glanced at each other and simultaneously exploded with laughter; the narrow escape was so sudden and unexpected that we were hysterical with relief.

"Kiss my butt! Ooowwww! Oowwwwwwwwwwww! Kiss my butt!" David screamed.

Crock wallowed in the river like a bag of discarded laundry. The others raced up to him. They cursed and shouted. One tossed a fence slat at us, but it careened away and tumbled into the water like a duck that had been shot out of the sky. Another man scooped a fist-sized rock from the river bottom and pitched it at us. The rock sailed close to my head and I flinched. The men cheered. They all started tossing rocks, and small geysers erupted around us. It was hard to paddle and dodge the rocks. One the size of a baseball brushed my shoulder, and two others struck the canoe and made a hollow ring. I heard a grunt and the canoe slowed. I turned and saw David curled forward, holding the back of his head with both hands, moaning. He dropped his paddle into the water. More rocks sailed past. David yelped and the men shouted gleefully. The side of my head suddenly exploded with a stinging, electric heat. I cupped my ear with my hand; a thin line of blood trickled down my forearm and dribbled off my elbow.

More rocks rained down, but none found their target. The lengthening distance between us destroyed their marksmanship. I paddled until we were hidden by the bend in the river. My lungs burned and I gulped air. David was still bent over and rubbing the back of his head.

"Are you OK?" I asked.

He lifted his head and gazed at me stupidly, like he had just woken from a deep sleep.

"David?"

22

I started to scramble back to him but froze when the canoe started rocking dangerously. I looked for a place to land, but there was only thick, rough brush. The river had narrowed, and we were funneling swiftly—very swiftly—into a dark tunnel. In no time, we plunged into its square opening. The tunnel was made of concrete and was about fifty yards long. I hunched over to avoid scraping my head on its low, coarse ceiling. The canoe bounced against slimy algae-covered walls. What were we traveling beneath? A road? A railway?

The current was racing and we reached the exit in moments. We squirted out, plunged down a rocky chute, and careered around a roaring curve. Paddling was useless; we were washed up against the outside bank, where a fallen tree lay in the river. The stump was facing upstream; it made a foaming, splashing breakwater. Scores of river-polished roots beckoned through the spray. *They look like dinosaur teeth*, I thought in the instant before we struck them sideways and capsized.

I tumbled from the canoe and plunged underwater. The current swept me under the half-sunken tree. Its branches snagged and clutched me. I thought of the many times I had been imprisoned under heavy surf at the beach. I held my breath. *I held on.*

I popped to the surface. The scuttled canoe wallowed nearby, as did bits of our gear.

"David!" I shouted as I spun around and searched for him. "David!"

A surge of panic jolted me, and I trembled.

"David!"

My eyes darted everywhere.

"David!"

I squinted at the stump and through the spray from the collision of river and tree. There, tumbling in the churning, roaring water, were our paddles, a plastic bag, my sweatshirt. And David's leg.

His pants were hung up on a root, and the rushing river was buffeting his submerged body against the tree.

I clawed my way out of the water and onto the bank. I tripped but kept going on my hands and knees. Regaining my feet, I raced to the tree and scrambled over it. I slipped on slick moss-covered bark. Jagged branches radiating from the trunk stabbed me. I dove over the stump, fell headlong through the roots—snapping the small ones and slithering through the others—and crashed into the water next to

David's leg. I tore him free and grasped his leg. We were sucked underwater and washed downstream. Another sharp branch seized David, but I muscled him free. We surfaced close to the bank, and I dragged David out of the water.

I shook him. He moaned and struggled to his hands and knees. I tried helping him but he pushed me away. His head hung like the end of a well-worn rope. Water and phlegm spewed from his mouth in racking, coarse coughs. White-green mucous streamed from his nose and collected above his lip. He wiped it away with the back of his hand.

I collapsed, rolled onto my back, and closed my eyes. My heart was racing, and I hoped lying still would calm it. David's hacking coughs lessened and finally ceased. I felt his hand on my shoulder, and I opened my eyes. David was on his knees beside me. His eyes were red-rimmed and he looked exhausted. I got to my knees and faced him. He leaned forward until his forehead was resting on my shoulder. I watched his back rise and fall as he took deep breaths. Finally, he lifted his head and pressed his forehead against mine.

"Score one for Steve," he whispered, the warmth of his breath caressing my face. "Thanks."

23

I wanted to get far away from Snake Landing and paddled hard while David rested in the front of the canoe. Three hours passed before I felt safe enough to stop at a small river town. I found a pay phone and called home, explaining to Dad that two weeks on the river was enough and that David wanted to come home and spend time with Mom. I didn't mention Crock. Dad promised to come for us and arrived six hours later. He was alone; Mom had stayed behind, he explained, to roast a turkey, David's favorite meal. Although we wouldn't return until midnight, Mom had still insisted on preparing the meal.

We threw our packs into the Country Squire and slid the canoe onto the roof.

"Better make sure this is properly anchored," Dad said. He trussed the canoe with so many ropes that it resembled some kind of weird hostage.

"Bet this canoe has a few stories to tell, huh boys?" Dad

asked as he tied the last knot, then petted the canoe as if it were the family dog. He smiled crookedly and eyed the bruises on our faces.

"Yeah," David replied. He smiled and slid into the station wagon's backseat. Dad looked at me, but I just shrugged and climbed into the front seat. Dad got behind the wheel, and, wordlessly, we drove away from the Susquehanna. An hour passed before David started entertaining Dad with tales of our time on the river, which he portrayed as a series of comic misadventures in which he was the butt of the joke, dubbing himself Loser of the River. He never mentioned Snake Landing or Crock.

We passed a sprawling magenta-colored diner. WOODY'S FAMOUS CHOW-DOWN RESTAURANT read its sign.

"We *gotta* stop here!" Dad declared with gusto, turning the car into a crowded parking lot.

Inside the restaurant, a young waitress directed us to a booth. Dad and David scanned the menu, but I couldn't keep my eyes off the waitress. I was mesmerized by the battle her uniform was waging to contain her shapely figure. Her hair was the color of a brightly polished trumpet, but I thought she was beautiful. As I watched her pour coffee for another customer, I felt Dad gently tap my shoulder.

"Son, it isn't polite to leer," he said quietly, almost whispering.

My face became warm.

"Yeah, that's Dad's job," David quickly added, and they burst into laughter.

I started to laugh, too, but hesitantly. I wasn't sure if I was included in the joke, and I felt better after Dad winked at me.

The waitress with the brassy hair took our order. Dad called her Darlin,' and she smiled; he left a big tip when we left.

We motored away from the diner and Dad asked, "Did you get her number? The waitress?"

"I tried," I joked. "But she was only interested in you."

"Yeah, Dad," David laughed. "Over-the-hill married guys turn her on!"

"Wiseasses," Dad groaned with mock displeasure.

Dad told stories about old girlfriends, growing up in the Depression, and his trip down the Susquehanna. David and I had heard most of them before, but they seemed more interesting now. We snacked on the candy and soda we had purchased at Woody's. Dad stopped on an empty country road and the three of us took a leak in the brush. It was nearly one o'clock when we returned home. Mom must have heard our arrival because she rushed out to greet us, dispensing tight hugs in age order: first me, then David, and finally Dad.

24

David threw his olive-drab duffel bag into the station wagon, then joined me in the backseat.

"All set?" Dad asked from the driver's seat. Mom sat beside Dad. She stared straight ahead and said nothing.

David nodded. We backed out of the driveway and motored down the street David and I had known since birth. The car was stuffy and silent. David leaned over the front seat, switched on the radio, and tuned it to music.

"Oh, no, not rock and roll!" Dad joked.

No one answered him.

"Should I stop for snacks?" he asked, and he turned to Mom. "Coffee?"

She shook her head.

We traveled the highway off Long Island and headed to McGuire Air Force Base in New Jersey. There we entered the parking lot of a modest one-story departure building set beside a long jet runway. A chartered airliner awaited David and one hundred other soldiers. The flight plan's twenty-three-hour itinerary would take them to California, Alaska, Japan, and, finally, Tan Son Nhut Air Force Base, Republic of Vietnam.

David removed his duffel bag from the car. It was hot and humid; sweat stained David's shirt.

"Need some help?" I asked.

He didn't say anything and threw the bag over his shoulder.

In the waiting room, soldiers in combat fatigues lolled across rows of high-backed, dark-stained wooden benches like the ones you might find in an old train station. The soldiers talked and joked. There were also about a dozen civilians. I guessed they were family or friends. I don't know why there were so few. Maybe they could only bear to make private good-byes at their homes. David disappeared for a few moments, I guess to tell whoever was in charge that he had arrived. When he returned, he leaned against a bench and watched the exit to the tarmac.

"These guys are marines. They're traveling as a unit," David said, nodding toward the fatigue-clad soldiers. "They must have come directly from their base. I'll be assigned to a unit in Nam."

Mom, Dad, and I found an empty bench and sat. Dad hunched over, rested his elbows on his knees, and looked down at the brown-speckled linoleum floor. Mom, straight-backed, stared forward, clutching her pocketbook in her lap with a grip tight enough to drive the blood from her hands. I sat for a moment but found it impossible to be still, so I got back to my feet and looked at the young soldiers around me. Seeing them reminded me of Felix and the carny crew.

The order was given to board the plane, and the crowd began to shuffle out.

"I'll call from California, if they let us off the plane," David said.

"We'll wait for your call. Take care of yourself," Dad replied, and they hugged. "Listen to what they tell you over there. You'll be OK," Dad said.

David turned to me, cupped the back of my neck with his hand and let go right away, and said, "See ya, Stevie."

Mom stood there. Silent. Eyes liquid. Hands in fists. David put his arms around her and squeezed.

"Take care, Mom. Love ya," he said, and then he left.

He walked across the tarmac, climbed a ramp, and disappeared into the plane. He never turned around. Mom watched him the whole time, then ran to the parking lot and vomited. We drove home and Dad went to work, just like it was an ordinary day. I hated him for that. I found Mom staring at a darkened TV screen, weeping. I hugged her and felt the anguished fluttering of her body.

David never called from California.

25

I tried to fit in at high school, but my efforts were failing. The football coach turned me down for the team and suggested soccer, which I joined and quit in short order. I just stunk at it. I quit choir, too. My grades slipped, and I had trouble making C's and D's. Mom and Dad weren't happy about any of it.

My fellow Toes, on the other hand, slipped into high school life as easily as an otter slides into a stream. Terry and J. M. made the football team, and Lip Man proved to have a natural talent for soccer, a team he joined only as a favor to me so that I would have a buddy on the squad. Scott loved his classes and occupied his after-school time in the biology lab, concocting his own experiments.

They didn't make a big deal about David. After his departure to Vietnam, Terry asked, "Did he leave?"

I nodded, and he reached out and touched my shoulder.

Lip Man regularly asked about David, but I didn't tell him much. I didn't like talking about it.

David sent us "spoken" letters on audiotape, and we sent him news the same way; none of us like to write. At first his messages were long, upbeat, and newsy: how steamy it was there, how he and three other replacements were helicoptered to a small base in the jungle, what a jerk his new sergeant was. But after a while, the messages shortened and the descriptions of the heat and landscape seemed forced. I sent him plenty of tapes, but he rarely responded.

After about two months, I got the "bad" tape that was addressed only to me.

"Hey, Steve," his tape began, his voice low and scratchy.

Bad stuff happened yesterday. We got ambushed and everything went crazy. I'm not sure what happened, and when I try to remember, it's hard to sort out. I was scared, really scared. Sergeant Priestly was everywhere, everywhere! Without him, we all would have been . . .

There was shooting and explosions and the noise, the noise was so loud! I couldn't even think, *it was so loud.*

Bad stuff was happening all around me, ya know? All of a sudden, a guy ran out of the bush at me and I . . . It just happened. *I didn't even aim, I just pointed and . . . and . . . Afterward, the other guys wanted me to come over and look, but I couldn't. . . .*

Three of our guys got wasted, too. One was a guy I first arrived with. I had to load his body bag onto a chopper. Don't tell Mom and Dad, OK?

When Mom asked about the tape, I told her it was nothing special and quickly hid it in my closet. I felt bad; tapes from David, and the television news, were the focus of her life.

At six each evening, she pulled a chair directly in front of the TV and spinned the dial between the different news shows, searching for the latest bit of information about Vietnam. Her body sagged when fighting was reported in David's area. She'd smile when battles were taking place elsewhere; had Mom decided that the war required a certain quota of death and another mother's tragedy was the price to be paid for David's survival? Mom got old while David was away, or so it seemed to me. She complained of being tired all the time, and the pleasure she once found in simple things like a good cup of coffee or a newly discovered antiques shop disappeared. Dad never seemed to pay any attention to the war or behave differently than he had when David was attending college. Only once did I hear him talk about David and Vietnam. He told a neighbor that his only fear was the widespread drug use among the soldiers and that David might return home a drug addict. *What a peckerhead*, I said to myself when I heard him say that.

One night I dreamed about Crock. In the dream, he *didn't* miss the canoe.

David had been in Vietnam for seven months when we

received word from him that he was working as a headquarters clerk.

"Priestly got me the job. It's really boring, but at least I'm
out of the bush," he said. "Priestly is great."

Mom cried. Dad squeezed my arm. We all felt better for
David.

I joined the track team, and my grades improved. I even
mustered the courage to ask Linda LaTorrance out on a date.
(She turned me down, saying she was dating an eleventh
grader.) There were even some days when I forgot David
was in Vietnam.

It was late in the afternoon on a rainy, gray Thursday,
and I was leaving school after track practice, when the coach,
Mr. Schill, called, "Steven—uh, *Steve.*"

"Your dad is on his way over to pick you up," he said.

Before I had time to wonder why Dad was home early
and needed to pick me up, Schill murmured, "Your brother.
Something about your brother."

26

David flew from an army hospital in Japan to Kennedy Airport in New York.

"David!" Dad roared when he saw him emerge from the airliner ramp.

Mom raced forward and threw her arms around him. Dad quickly joined them and stroked David's back. I was off to the side until Dad noticed and took my hand and pulled me into the huddle. We stood that way for a long, long time, until Mom finally released David and dabbed the tears away from her eyes. With a choked voice, she asked him if he had been eating well, were there clothes to be laundered, was everything OK, was everything *really* OK? As she spoke, she caressed the side of his head; the rocket that had struck David's office had burst his eardrums, and there was some question whether his hearing would ever completely return. But we knew better than to complain: two soldiers had been killed in the same attack, a fate David would have suffered had he not been shuffling papers behind file cabinets at that horrible moment.

David absently shook his head and moved over so that I stood between him and them. His shoulders drooped and there were dark shadows beneath his eyes.

"Hey, Steve," he said, reaching out and cupping the back of my neck.

"Hey, David," I answered.

We drove home and enjoyed a cake from Spiro's Bakery that had WELCOME HOME, DAVID! emblazoned in blue icing across it.

After Mom and Dad went to sleep, David and I sat in the kitchen.

"How's school?" David finally asked after a few moments of uncomfortable silence.

"It only half sucks," I replied, making David chuckle. "Do you have any plans?"

"I dunno. Go back to college, I guess. Or work. I dunno." He looked glum.

"How about the Susquehanna? Cooperstown to Havre de Grace," I said. And he brightened.

"It'll make men of us," he joked, and we both laughed. I reached over and held his hand. He didn't let go.

We talked about the Susquehanna, about Crock and the morning at Snake Landing. Our shared memories carried us, their path bending and turning and delivering us to unexpected places.

Like a river.